GHOSTLY ISSUES

A HARPER HARLOW MYSTERY BOOK TWO

LILY HARPER HART

HARPERHART PUBLICATIONS

ONE

"Have you ever considered that you might be the world's biggest pain in the ass?"

Harper Harlow narrowed her blue eyes and glared at her best friend Zander Pritchett, practically daring him to make things worse. "Have you ever considered that I can beat you up even though I'm a woman?"

Zander shrugged, unruffled. "Whether that is or is not true – and it's not because I work out so much I can bench press a car ... that's right, a car – it doesn't change the fact that you're a pain in the ass."

Zander ducked as a crystal vase hurtled toward the wall he pressed himself against, seemingly coming from nowhere, and brushed his hand through his dark hair to clear off the shattered glass. "Case in point ... instead of just setting out the dreamcatcher on the main floor and enticing the ghost to us, you insisted that going on a hunt was the best way to do things.

"Look at us now, Harper! We're stuck on the third floor with a really hacked off ghost throwing vases at us," he continued. "Do you still think you had the better idea?"

Harper made a face that would've been comical under different circumstances. "Are we dead?"

"If that's one of the options for how this day is going to go, then I don't want to play this game one second longer," Zander announced, crossing his arms over his chest. "I'm really mad at you!"

"If we tried to catch the ghost downstairs we would've risked someone walking into the middle of what we were doing," Harper said, sounding pragmatic for all intents and purposes, but Zander knew better. "This way was safer for the general public."

"Why would someone walk into the building off the street? It's empty. That's why we're here."

Harper wrinkled her nose. "You don't know that. You can't underestimate people or predict why they do anything. You know that. Stop being purposely dramatic."

Zander grabbed Harper's shoulders and for a second she thought he was going to shake her. Instead he pushed her to the other side of the hallway and covered her head when a chunk of something – it was hard to tell what it was in the rundown hotel they currently found themselves working – thudded against the wall she'd been leaning against.

"Thanks," Harper said, exhaling heavily.

Zander rolled his eyes. "I love you, Harper. You're my best friend in the world. That doesn't mean I won't kill you."

"You just saved me!"

"That's because I'm manly and strong and like to tell people I'm a hero," Zander countered. "I have murderous tendencies, too. You know that. If this was a comic book, we both know I could go easily go either way to superhero or super villain. It all depends on which character has the better wardrobe."

What Harper knew was that Zander was really a big ball of fluff – especially where she was concerned – and he really only complained to hear himself talk when he was nervous. An enraged ghost – one who most certainly did not want to be displaced from his earthly dwelling – was enough to make anyone nervous. Zander was a super man, but he wasn't a super hero (no matter what he told the men he dated).

The best friends and fellow ghost hunters – co-owners of Ghost

Hunters, Inc. (GHI to those in the inner loop) were working a job at The Regency, a former Detroit hotel that was up for sale. The owners couldn't unload it thanks to a pesky soul who refused to leave – or let them fix anything up – so for lack of anything better to do, they hired the dynamic duo to cleanse the property. It wasn't going well.

"Hey, guys, I have some background on who we think this ghost is." Molly Parker's voice crackled over Harper and Zander's ear buds. As a twenty-one-year-old intern, she was all enthusiasm and bravado, even though Harper insisted on keeping her at a safe distance these days. She'd almost died two weeks before thanks to a murderous college classmate, and Harper wasn't convinced she was over the ordeal. Molly kept insisting she was fine, but the girl was hyper-vigilant and jumpy, and Harper refused to rush Molly on her road to recovery. With that in mind, Harper insisted Molly do research in The Regency's main office while their tech guy, Eric Tyler, monitored everything he could from afar and kept an eye on her at the same time.

"What do you have, Molly?"

"One Dennis Dombrowski was murdered by another guest on the third floor in 1982," Molly said. "Apparently he caught the guest trying to strangle a hooker and intervened. The cops showed up in time to save the hooker, but Dombrowski died thanks to a knife wound to the throat."

"Nice," Harper muttered.

"So this guy was a hero and now he's haunting the place where he was murdered?" Zander asked. "That's kind of sad. Maybe we should tell him he's a hero and that will calm him down. He'd probably be happy to move to the other side if he knew he was a hero. He probably thinks he died without recognition."

An oil painting flew off a nearby wall and slammed into Zander's arm, causing him to howl in surprise rather than pain. "Hey! I'm on your side, Dennis. I'm a hero, too. There's no need to get all huffy. It was just a suggestion."

Harper pursed her lips to keep from laughing. "It was a good suggestion," she said, patting Zander's arm.

"Don't placate me." Zander moved so he could peer down the corridor. They were in the main hallway while Dennis zoomed around another, the two hallways meeting in a "T." Dennis was running out of things to throw, and it was unclear if that was a good or bad thing. "I wish I could see ghosts."

Harper could see ghosts since she was a child, her own grandfather coming to say goodbye to her before he passed over to the other side. As her best friend, Zander readily believed her stories when they were little. Harper had no idea if it was merely a show of solidarity or true faith, but when he agreed to start a ghost hunting business with her after college, she realized just how lucky she was in the friend department. Even though he bravely stood by her in case after case, he had a tendency to display frayed nerves when things hit the fan. Harper sensed that now – even though Dennis the less-than-friendly ghost hadn't managed to stumble across a fan to throw in their direction yet.

"Do you want to go downstairs and help Eric and Molly?"

Zander scowled. "Are you insinuating I'm a fraidy cat?"

That was one of their childhood taunts. "No. I … you seem nervous?"

"Of course I'm nervous, Harp! There's a pissed off ghost throwing vases … and paintings … and really ugly decorations at us. Who wouldn't be nervous in that situation?" Zander's hands landed on his narrow hips. "That doesn't mean I'm going anywhere. We're in this together."

Harper's smile was rueful. "I wasn't saying that you're not brave. I …."

"Of course I'm brave!" Zander's voice was shrill. "I'm your knight in shining linen!"

Harper couldn't remember what they were arguing about. That was a regular occurrence, so she decided to change tactics. "Okay, I think we need to handle this like adults instead of children."

"So you don't want me to scream and tell you that 'I'm rubber and you're glue'?" Zander deadpanned. "Is that what you're telling me?"

"Sarcasm is the refuge of the weak," Harper countered.

Zander exaggerated his handsome face into a grotesque "well duh" expression. "That must be why you're the most sarcastic person I know!"

"Hey, kids? Do you want to hold off on the playground spat until after you've helped the ghost move on to the other side?" Eric's voice was smooth as it passed into Harper and Zander's ear buds. "I know this is a life or death argument – like all of them are – but I think the ghost should be our priority. In case you forgot, the building owner is waiting in the lobby and he doesn't look thrilled with all the noise you two are making up there."

"Oh, screw him," Zander muttered. "There's a reason why I make them sign a contract before we even start these jobs. That guy has 'tool' written all over him."

Harper snorted. "You just don't like his suit."

"It's polyester," Zander shot back. "The only person who likes a polyester suit is a tool ... and a prostitute. You know it and I know it, too. Don't bother arguing with me. You know I'm right."

Harper knew better than to argue with Zander about the complexity of unbreathable fabrics. "Fine. We need to come up with a plan here. Eric, do you have anything on the thermal camera we set up by the elevator when we came up?"

"Um ... hold on," Eric muttered and Harper could hear his fingers flying across a keyboard. "I see you and Zander. You look like you're pressed against a wall. You're the only hot spots on the floor."

"I'll bet I look hotter," Zander muttered.

Eric ignored him. "There's a cold spot down the adjacent hallway," he said. "It's ... doing something ... next to the wall. If I didn't know better I would think it's trying to pull a painting off or something."

"Oh, well good," Zander snapped. "That will be the second painting it's thrown at us. It's a good thing they're ugly because otherwise it would be a crime against the artistic world. Those paintings are already a crime against the artistic world, so we're doing two good deeds today."

"I kind of liked the one of the forest," Harper hedged. "It had personality."

Zander patted the top of Harper's blond head. "Yes, it had the personality of a drunken sailor on shore leave."

"You're so funny," Harper said, jerking her head away from Zander's persistent hand. "Come on. We need to work together and do this."

"What do you suggest?"

"I'm going to run out into the other hallway but move away from the ghost," Harper replied, not missing a beat. "You're going to wait until Eric tells you the ghost is moving and throw the dreamcatcher out at the exact right time. Then, when the ghost moves in to attack me – or throw something new – he's going to move right over the trap."

"Yes, that sounds lovely," Zander said calmly. "And because all ghosts float exactly where we want them to, what happens when the ghost tries to kill you and there's nowhere to hide?"

"Then … ." Harper broke off, conflicted. She was already in a foul mood. If a ghost wanted to attack her, well, at least she would have something to take her pent up anger out on. "This is going to work. We don't need a backup plan."

"Hold it right there," Zander said, snagging the back of Harper's shirt before she could move away from him. "I know what you're doing. You want to burn off all that excess energy that's been building since Jared left town. I don't think killing yourself is the way to go."

Well, that was hitting below the belt, Harper internally seethed. Jared Monroe was Whisper Cove's newest police officer. He was sexy, handsome, and brash – all things Harper liked in a man. After a week of flirting, one hot kiss, and the promise of a first date, Jared followed it all up by fleeing town to help his mother with a broken leg.

Harper didn't begrudge Jared a family emergency. In fact, there was something appealing about a man who doted on his mother. What wasn't appealing was the fact that Jared hadn't bothered to call … or text … or even poke her on Facebook for the entire ten days he'd been gone.

"I have no intention of killing myself," Harper seethed. "I know what I'm doing. How many times have I done this?"

Zander rolled his eyes dramatically. "More than I can count."

"Do you have so little faith in me that you think I would purposely put myself in danger because I got dumped?"

"You didn't get dumped, Harp," Zander argued. "He's taking care of his mother. That's a good thing. That means when you get old and dumpy he'll take care of you, too."

Harper narrowed her eyes to dangerous slits. "What did you just say?"

"I love you more than life itself," Zander said, pressing a kiss to her forehead. "Go and do your thing. I'll be right here. If things get out of control, though …."

Harper knew he had absolutely nowhere to go with that statement so he pretended he didn't leave it hanging in the ether. "I love you, too. Let's do this." She clapped her hands together and moved out toward the second hallway, casting one more look in Zander's direction. "You'll take care of me when I'm old, right?"

Zander was nonplussed. "Oh, honey, we're going to rule the retirement community," he said. "Now … be careful. I'll have absolutely no one to love if you die on me."

Harper's expression softened. "I'll never die on you. In fact … we can die together."

Zander made a face. "Yeah, I'm never dying," he said. "At some point you're going to have to go first. By then you'll be too addled to care, though. That's how I always picture it anyway."

"Well, that's something to look forward to, isn't it?"

TWO

"Do you remember when I said that we were going to rule the retirement center when we were old and gray?" Zander asked three hours later, leaning over Harper's desk at their office in Whisper Cove with a disgusted look on his face.

Harper grimaced as she lifted her leg and studied the torn knee of her blue jeans. The takedown was a little rougher than she imagined. Still, at the end of the day, they accomplished their task and secured payment. She had no idea why Zander was so irritated. "Yes. It was a beautiful sentiment."

"I take it back," Zander hissed. "I don't want to be friends with you when I'm old. You're going to make all of my hair fall out if you keep up with your current attitude – and no one wants that!"

"I think you would look hot with a bald head," Molly offered, settling in the chair across from Harper's desk. "You would look like Lex Luthor … only hot."

Zander couldn't decide if he wanted to preen under the compliment or continue yelling. He opted to do both. "Of course I would be sexy with a bald head," he said. "No one is disputing that. My head is very smooth and being bald would make me look distinguished. I still don't want to be bald. All that scalp moisturizing would be way too much upkeep."

"Says the guy who waxes his chest," Harper muttered.

"Don't push me, Harp," Zander warned, swiveling so he was facing his best friend again. "Why did you do it?"

Harper pretended she didn't understand the question. "Do what?"

"Don't act innocent with me. You know darned well what I'm talking about."

"I'm afraid I can't recall doing anything that would upset you," Harper said, gritting her teeth as she tenderly touched the skin around her scraped knee. "Molly, could you get me the first aid kit?"

Molly obediently nodded, her bright blue hair bobbing. Molly changed her hair color – and style – on a regular basis. She was threatening a Mohawk – which Zander vetoed because he thought it was an affront to hairstyles of the past, present, and future – but the blue color was a recent change. Harper thought it washed her skin out, but it wasn't her place to voice that. Molly wanted to feel in control of something – after being drugged, locked in a car trunk, and left for dead caused her to feel control over nothing – so she was being bolder with her look. Harper thought it was a healthy way to rebel.

"I'm not joking with you, Harper," Zander said, pounding his fist against the top of the desk. "You ran out into that hallway and the ghost avoided the dreamcatcher trap after I threw it – like I told you would happen – and then you were left exposed."

The dreamcatchers were an invention that allowed Harper to expend her limited mental energies – she only had special power where ghosts were concerned – and direct them to the other side. She had no idea how she did it, learning the first time via a happy accident, but now it was a regular offering at GHI. She enjoyed doing it because, however fleeting, the glimpse at a better place always warmed her. Zander didn't understand because he couldn't see the other world.

"I'm fine," Harper said. "You can see me here, can't you? I'm not dead."

"You got slammed into a wall and the only reason you're still here and not buried under a mountain of terribly tacky 1970s decorations is because I ran out into the hallway and threw the dreamcatcher directly on top of you," Zander argued. "If we stuck to your plan you'd probably be dead."

"I'm fine. You're fine. Everyone is fine."

Zander threw up his hands in frustration. "I know why you're doing this," he said. "You're feeling reckless because you think Jared dumped you and walked away. That's not what happened. You need to stop feeling sorry for yourself and get over it!"

"I told you not to bring up *his* name," Harper hissed. "I don't want to talk about Jared Monroe."

"Oh, Harp, the only thing you want to do is fixate on Jared," Zander said. "I can't wait until he gets back to town and you realize just how much you've been acting like a lunatic. It's so ... annoying."

"You're annoying!"

"I'm rubber and you're glue ... ."

"Okay," Molly said, holding up her hands to still the argument and stepping between Zander and the desk. "Why don't you go and ... help Eric with the tech from today's job, Zander?"

Zander frowned. "I'm nowhere near done yelling at Harper yet."

"You guys live together, though," Molly pointed out. "Wouldn't it be more fun to yell at her when you're home? I know it would be more fun for me."

"How? You don't live with us. You wouldn't be able to hear it."

"Exactly," Molly said. "Just ... leave me alone with Harper for a few minutes. I'll bandage up her knee while you two cool down. In a half hour you won't even remember why you were sniping at each other."

"I'll remember," Zander announced, moving toward the back of the office. "I'll remember forever the day that I saved Harper from certain death and she didn't even thank me for it."

"Thank you, Zander!" Harper screeched at his back.

"You're welcome!"

. . .

"**THAT** WAS ... INTERESTING," Molly said a few minutes later, wisely opting to give Harper space to collect her breath – and rein in her anger – before treating her knee. "Are you going to kick me if I try to help you?"

Harper frowned. "Of course not."

Molly arched a challenging eyebrow. "Are you sure? You just kicked Zander and he was trying to help you. I'm not in the mood to be kicked."

Harper sighed, resigned, and leaned back in her chair so she could study the ceiling. "I'm sorry if you and Eric are tired of listening to Zander and me fight. It's just ... we're going through a rough patch right now."

"I don't think Zander is the one having a rough patch," Molly pointed out. "I think you're the one having a rough patch because of the whole Jared thing."

"I don't want to hear his name!"

"Well, I'm not in middle school so I don't play that game," Molly countered, dabbing some peroxide on a cotton ball and gingerly pressing it to Harper's torn skin. "When was the last time you had a tetanus shot? I don't want you to get lockjaw and die. Well ... the lockjaw actually wouldn't be so bad right about now."

"I had one six months ago. I'm fine."

"You keep saying that you're fine, but I'm not sure you really are," Molly said. "In fact, if I had to put a name to what you're feeling, I think the correct one would be hurt."

"That's preposterous."

Molly pursed her lips and continued cleaning Harper's wound. "Zander loves you more than anything and he's really upset," she said. "What you did today was stupid. We all saw it. I have no idea why you're denying it."

"I ... something had to be done." Harper was flustered. "What should we have done?"

"Figured out another way to draw Dennis into the dreamcatcher," Molly replied, not missing a beat. "There were several other options. You could've tossed the dreamcatcher out into the middle of the hallway and then raced back to be with Zander, for one. Instead you decided to take on an angry ghost by yourself, and the only rationale I can come up with is that you wanted to … feel … something."

"Are you taking psychology classes again this semester?"

Now it was Molly's turn to frown. "You've been lashing out at people for days now," she said. "You can say it's not because of Jared, but we all know it is. Maybe if you talk about it … ."

Harper cut Molly off. "There's nothing to talk about," she said. "We shared exactly one kiss and two flirty calls and then he left town. It's not like he was my boyfriend. I have absolutely no reason to be angry with him. He didn't promise me anything."

"That doesn't mean that cutting off contact between the two of you didn't hurt your feelings," Molly chided. "It's okay to have feelings. It's okay to be upset. You're entitled to feel how you feel. Jared made a stupid decision. That doesn't mean he doesn't like you."

"I know exactly what it means," Harper said. "It means he's changed his mind."

Molly knit her eyebrows together. "How do you figure that?"

"Once he spent a few days away he realized I was too much work and he doesn't want to date the freak who can see ghosts. It's pretty obvious what happened."

"I think you're making a very broad leap there," Molly said. "Maybe he was just busy taking care of his mother. Did you ever think of that?"

"Yes. That's what got me through the first five days. The second five days were different. I couldn't keep lying to myself that he was too busy to send a ten-second text."

"I … ." Molly didn't know what to say. "Harper, you know that I saw you and Jared together the day it … happened, right?" She didn't want to talk about her ordeal so she cleared her throat and moved on. "He didn't seem like a guy who was going to change his mind. In fact, he seemed thrilled to be around you. He was excited. I think you should wait to talk to him before you convince yourself of the worst possible scenario."

"Whatever," Harper said, crossing her arms over her chest. "I know the truth. You don't want to hurt my feelings so you're telling me what you think I want to hear. I'm over Jared Monroe. I barely liked him anyway."

Molly didn't believe that for a second. She'd never seen her boss show interest in a man until Jared walked into her life. She didn't think now was the time to press the issue, though. "Well, if that's your decision, then I'm not going to try and change your mind," she said.

"That's good. It can't be changed."

"Do you want to hear about me?" Molly asked, her eyes sparkling.

"Always," Harper said. "What's new with you?"

"I've finally decided to ask Eric out," Molly replied. "I'm going to do it today ... or maybe tomorrow if I can't get my courage up."

Harper's blue eyes widened. "Seriously? I thought you were going to let him come to you. That's a big change in strategy." Molly had boasted a crush on Eric since the first day she was hired as an intern. Eric, in turn, had a crush on Harper and barely knew Molly was alive – except when she irritated him. Everyone ignored the dueling crush situation and pretended it wasn't happening ... until now apparently.

"If I've learned anything from what happened to me it's that I don't want to wait for Eric to come to me," Molly replied. "I'm going to ask him out. If he doesn't want to do it, well, at least I'll know and I can move on. I don't want to live in limbo. I want to try to find someone who will make me happy."

"Good for you."

"**WHY** IS HARPER BEING SUCH A PILL?" Eric asked, moving to Zander's side and watching Harper and Molly chat in the next room. "She's been extremely crabby the past few days."

"I would say it's PMS, but that was last week," Zander answered, causing Eric to grimace and squirm. "She's upset and taking it out on me because she knows I'll always forgive her."

"You don't look like you want to forgive her."

"It's not on top of my to-do list right now," Zander admitted. "I know she's hurt and upset, but ... she's being a real B-I-T-C-H."

"Why are you spelling?" Eric asked, glancing around.

"Harper doesn't like it when I say that word in conjunction with her attitude," Zander explained. "I started spelling it when we were in high school sometimes to make her laugh. Now I kind of want to punch her with it."

Eric raised his eyebrows. "This must be serious. You two never fight for more than a few hours."

"That's because she's turning into the Devil."

"Do you really think it's about that cop dumping her?" Eric asked, his eyes trained on Harper as she and Molly whispered to one another. "Do you think she's ... vulnerable?"

Zander flicked Eric's ear. "I think you're barking up the wrong tree," he said. "I know that look on your face. Harper and Jared didn't break up. Jared had to leave town to take care of his mother. Harper is making a mountain out of a molehill. She always does. The second she sees Jared again they're going to be smacking lips and rattling headboards. Mark my words."

"So maybe I should ask her out before Jared gets back to town," Eric mused. "Now could be the perfect time for me to slide in and charm her."

"You're an idiot," Zander said. "No offense, man, but you don't have a shot."

"Why not?" Eric looked pained.

"Because Harper has a thing for Jared," Zander answered. "I haven't seen her react to a man in that manner in ... years. In fact, everything else I've ever seen her do regarding a man has been lame in comparison to Jared."

"Yes, but ... if we go out she might realize Jared is all wrong for her," Eric suggested. "She'll realize I'm the one for her and forget all about him."

"I like you, Eric," Zander said, choosing his words carefully. "You're not right for Harper, though. Jared is right for her. She's going to realize that the second he comes back to town."

"Not if I go out with her first."

"She won't go out with you," Zander said. "She'll find a nice way to let you down easy and then everyone will be uncomfortable around the office for weeks after you do it. I'm begging you, man, just … don't."

"You don't know," Eric protested. "She could have a secret thing for me."

"We live together. She doesn't."

"But … ."

Zander wagged a finger in front of Eric's face. "Don't even think about it," he said. "You're going to end up crushed and she's going to feel awful about shooting you down. This is a losing situation for everyone. If you want to ask someone out, ask Molly. She adores you."

"Molly is a kid," Eric countered. "She's nice enough, but she's not my type."

"That's exactly how Harper feels about you."

Eric mulled the words and then squared his shoulders. "I'm going to do it. I'm going to do it right now and prove you wrong."

Zander lunged at Eric's elbow to still him and missed. "Don't do it," he hissed.

Thankfully, Harper's dramatic announcement to Molly put the kibosh on everything so Zander didn't have to think of a way to fake a fire alarm before Eric walked twenty feet.

"I am completely done with men," Harper said, her voice carrying. "I'm going to set the next one who asks me out on fire. That's how done I am with men."

Eric swiveled quickly and moved back in Zander's direction. "Now probably isn't the best time."

"That's a wise choice."

THREE

"There he is, my wayward partner. I thought you changed your mind about moving to Whisper Cove and decided to stay on the west side of the state."

Mel Kelsey leaned back in his desk chair, his fingers linked as he rested his head against the palms of his hands.

Jared shot his partner a rueful smile and moved toward his desk. "I'm sorry for dropping everything on you the way I did," he said. "My mother was in a lot of pain, though, and my sister was on a business trip so she couldn't help. I didn't know what else to do."

"It's fine," Mel said, waving off Jared's apology. "We haven't had much going on. Everything has been quiet. I told you that having a murder your first week on the job was a fluke. The only thing happening last week was Donna Frisbee's mental breakdown."

"Who is Donna Frisbee?" Jared sat at his desk and started rummaging through the stack of accumulated paperwork and messages.

"She's one of the big social ladies in the area," Mel explained. "She fights with all the other social ladies. She turned up naked in the downtown square one day last week."

Jared arched an eyebrow. "Naked?"

"Well, she had on garter belts and nothing else. It was quite the sight."

"How old is she?"

"Seventy-five."

Jared made a face. "Nice. That's going to give me nightmares."

"She had a gun, too," Mel added. "She was looking for her husband. The sad thing is Big Bart died about twenty years ago. We took her over to that mental hospital in Mount Clemens and they're running some tests."

"Well, I'm sorry to hear that," Jared said, although his grin said otherwise. "At least the talk of the town wasn't murder or something truly awful."

"Yes. You look broken up about it," Mel teased. "So, why did you come to the office today? I thought you were due back tomorrow."

"Well, I thought I would get a start on all of this paperwork," Jared replied. "I also thought it would give me an excuse to be in town so I could stop at Harper's house on my way home. I want to surprise her."

Mel snickered, causing Jared to shift a wary look in his direction.

"What was that?" Jared asked.

"What?"

"You cackled like a witch there when I mentioned Harper," Jared pressed. "What's going on?"

"Why do you think anything is going on?" Mel asked, faux innocence and light practically wafting off of him. As Whisper Cove's longest serving cop, he was up on all of the hamlet's gossip. He was also Zander's favorite uncle, and he knew a thing or two about Harper's state of mind that Jared was obviously missing.

"Did something happen to Harper?" Jared asked, leaning forward. "I ... she's okay, isn't she?"

"Last time I heard – which was about an hour ago – the only thing wrong with Harper Harlow is her attitude," Mel replied, holding his hand up to caution Jared about getting ahead of himself. "Well, that's not entirely true. I guess something went wrong at their ghost-busting extravaganza down in Detroit today. She just skinned her knee, though."

"See, your tone tells me something else is going on," Jared said. "I don't like the look on your face."

"You're not the first person to tell me that."

"I'm going to be the last if you don't tell me what's going on," Jared threatened. "I'm worried now. Maybe I should go over to her house instead of playing games with you."

"I think that's a good way to get yourself shot," Mel said, enjoying the power he had over his younger partner. Harper's bad mood had been Zander's favorite gossip topic for days. Since Zander enjoyed gossiping with his mother – and his mother happened to be Mel's favorite sister – that meant Mel was up on all of Harper's meltdowns and shenanigans. He'd known Harper since she was a child. He'd seen her vicious streak up close and personal when she wanted revenge on someone.

"I don't understand what you're saying," Jared admitted, his frustration showing. "Why would I get shot if I go to see Harper?"

"Because she's not speaking to you."

Jared frowned. "Why?"

"She's mad as a zombie without human intestines to munch on," Mel replied, tapping his fingers on his desk. He didn't know Jared well yet, but he was enjoying sampling as many methods as possible to torture the young police officer.

"How is that even possible?" Jared asked, confused. "She was in a good mood when I left. I mean ... she wasn't happy that we were going to have to delay our first date ... but she was fine."

"That was ten days ago."

"Thanks. I'm so glad to know you can count." Jared's tone was snarky and irritated. He had no idea what he could've possibly done to upset Harper.

"Son, as much as I'm enjoying this, I have to ask you an honest question now," Mel said. "The thing is ... well ... I've been hearing a lot of gossip because Harper has been taking her mood out on Zander. My nephew and Harper have always been co-dependent, but he can't take it when she's upset ... and right now she's really upset."

"At me?" Jared's voice was unnaturally squeaky. "I haven't done a thing to upset her. I swear I ... ." He broke off, racking his brain. "I haven't done anything to upset Harper. If she's saying I've done something to her, well, she's mistaken."

Mel licked his lips. "Well, let's retrace your steps," he said, enjoying the game. In truth, he'd been bored during Jared's absence. Whisper Cove wasn't known as a hotbed of illegal activity. At least with Jared back he could torture his partner to break up the afternoon ennui. "What did she say to you the last time you called her?"

Jared faltered. "I ... well ... ." Jared pressed the heel of his hand against his forehead, not stopping until he dragged it completely through the top of his dark hair. "I didn't talk to her while I was out of town."

Mel feigned surprise. "What? I thought you liked her."

"I do like her!"

"Then why didn't you call her for ten days?" Mel asked.

"I ... my mother was hurt and ... um ... crap." Jared realized too late what he'd done.

"Well, let's not panic," Mel cautioned, refusing to let go of the game. "I'm sure you texted her, right?"

Jared dejectedly shook his head.

"Messaged her on Facebook?"

"I didn't do anything," Jared said. "I ... ." He made a disgusted sound in the back of his throat. "What is she saying?"

"Oh, well, she's saying a whole heck of a lot," Mel said, delighted with Jared's hangdog expression.

"Just ... lay it on me," Jared said. "I need to know what I'm up against if I'm going to get her to forgive me."

"First off, I think you should probably know that Harper is hurt more than anything else," Mel said, sobering. "She's not used to dating. She hasn't done it in a long time ... not since Quinn."

Quinn Jackson was Harper's last serious boyfriend. He'd died in a car accident years before and his body was never recovered. Jared knew the story. He knew how upset Harper was thinking his ghost wandered the woods looking for closure. He did not want to be the reason for causing her more pain.

"Harper is taking out her anger on Zander – and he's mean as a rabid raccoon right now, too – but Zander told his mother that Harper is really hurt," Mel continued. "She doesn't want anyone to know she's hurt, though, so she's being mean."

"Mean how?"

Mel shrugged. "You'll have to ask Zander for specifics," he said. "I know there was some incident with an angry ghost and putting herself in danger even though Zander told her not to do whatever she did. Apparently he had to step in and save her life – although he claims he saves her life every single day they go out, so that could be an exaggeration."

"I don't understand this," Jared admitted. "If she's so upset, why didn't she call me?"

"Why didn't you call her?"

"I didn't think it was a big deal," Jared shot back. "We're not even technically a couple yet. I didn't want to seem pathetic and call her four times a day."

"So you combated that by not calling her once in ten days? That sounds like a great way to go."

Jared scowled. "I didn't want her to think I was weak."

"No, you didn't want to cede the power position in the relationship," Mel corrected. "There's a difference."

"I don't even know what that means."

"That's because you haven't dated much either."

"I've dated tons of women!"

Mel rolled his eyes. "You know Harper tells Zander everything, right? And Zander tells his mother everything. So either you lied to Harper – which I'm going to have to tell my sister because my family is loyal to Harper more than you – or you really haven't dated all that much. Which is it?"

"Well, great," Jared huffed, crossing his arms over his chest as embarrassment washed over him.

"You wanted Harper to be the one to call you because that meant she missed you and you could have the power in the relationship," Mel said. "The problem is that it wasn't Harper's place to call you in this particular situation.

"You were the one to leave town to take care of your mother," he continued. "The polite thing for Harper to do was wait for you to contact her when everything was settled and you had a moment. You never did that."

"But ... ."

Mel shook his head to cut Jared off before he got a full head of steam. "She made excuses for you the first five days," he said. "I don't think she was sitting by the phone and waiting for you to call, but Zander says every day that passed and you didn't call was like a knife to the heart. Would it have really hurt you to call the girl once?"

Jared's heart rolled. He'd never considered it from Harper's point of view. He'd been waiting for her to call him. He understood disappointment. He felt it every night when she didn't call. "I ... made a mistake," he said finally. "After the first few days when she didn't call I realized she wasn't going to call. By then I felt like an idiot and it was too hard to call. I thought we would just make up for lost time when I saw her again."

"Yes, well, she doesn't want to see you right now," Mel said. "She's too hurt and if she sees you she's going to explode all over you."

Jared couldn't help but grin at the mental picture.

"Not in that way, you pervert," Mel hissed. "She's genuinely depressed. That shouldn't make you happy."

"That doesn't make me happy," Jared argued. "I just ... I missed her. I know it seems weird to say it because I don't know her all that well, but I got used to seeing her face. I was looking forward to going over there and hanging out with her tonight."

"You know Zander lives there, too, right?" Mel asked dryly.

"Yes, well, I was going to lock Zander in his bedroom ... or bribe him to go away ... ." Jared tugged on the ends of his hair, frustrated. "I screwed this up already. That has to be a record."

"The good news for you is that Harper is a forgiving girl," Mel said. "The bad news for you is that she lashes out when she's upset. You're going to have to find a way to sneak past her anger and get at her heart."

Jared licked his lips. "I don't suppose you have any suggestions, do you?"

"When dealing with women, I've found begging works like a charm."

"I would rather not beg," Jared admitted. "Then I'll really lose power – and self-respect – where she's concerned. I would like to make up without losing my pride."

"Well, in that case, I would suggest flowers and chocolate. They're clichés for a reason. Women love both of them."

"Does she have a favorite flower?"

"I have no idea," Mel replied. "If I remember right, she and Zander had some huge blowout about acceptable flowers once. I can't remember who won that argument, though. If I were you I'd go with the classic roses – red, not pink – and get some of those expensive chocolates with caramel in the center."

"Does she like caramel?"

Mel shrugged. "I do. Why wouldn't she?"

Jared sighed, resigned. "Okay. Flowers and chocolate it is. Tell me why I don't want pink roses, though?"

"Pink roses mean friendship. Is that the type of message you're trying to send? Men who send pink roses never get past the friend stage. I don't think that's what you ultimately want."

"Definitely not," Jared muttered. "So red roses and chocolate … I think I can handle that."

"You also might want to duck," Mel added.

"Duck?"

"She throws a punch like a man when she wants to," Mel said. "She's got a hell of a right cross. She knocked Zander out when they were teenagers and he told her she had wide hips and should never wear a pencil skirt because she could be mistaken as a crossdresser from behind."

Jared laughed. He couldn't help himself. "I'll cover my face to be on the safe side."

"Oh, and one other thing," Mel said, his eyes sparkling. "Try being honest with her. If you tell her you were scared to call her because you didn't want to look pathetic she'll probably understand that because she felt the same way."

"I hope you're right," Jared said. "I would hate to lose her before I really get her."

"Let's hope that doesn't happen, shall we? I'd like to see the girl smile ... and you seem to make her smile when you're not being a dope."

"I'd like to see her smile, too," Jared said. "That's what I missed the most."

FOUR

"This is nice," Zander said, licking his ice cream cone and lifting his face toward the sun as he walked down Main Street with Harper later in the afternoon.

"It is," Harper agreed, munching on her own ice cream cone.

The duo lapsed into amiable silence. Even when they were fighting they were comfortable with one another.

"It's a nice day," Zander said, opting for the most innocuous conversation topic he could think of. "I love this time of year. It's warm enough to forget winter and our crappy spring, but not hot enough to sweat yet."

Harper's eyes flashed. "Is this what we're really going to talk about?"

"What's wrong with this conversation?"

"The weather doesn't really whip me into a verbal frenzy."

"No, that would be your idiotic approach to going after ghosts," Zander shot back.

"Just let it go!"

"You let it go!"

Harper felt helpless. "I ... ." She knew what she wanted to say and yet she couldn't force the apology out of her mouth.

Zander's nostrils flared when he turned toward his lifelong best friend. "I can't take much more of this fighting," he said. "You're the love of my life, Harp, but you're killing me right now."

Harper's face was miserable when she finally raised her eyes to Zander. "I know. I'm sorry. I don't know what's wrong with me."

"I know exactly what's wrong with you, but you won't admit that's what's wrong with you so we're stuck in an endless loop," Zander said. "Just … admit it."

"I can't."

"Why not?"

"Because if I admit that I'm upset about Jared not calling it's the same thing as admitting I'm some pathetic … girl … who wraps her self-worth up in a man," Harper said. "I promised never to do that."

"Oh, stuff it," Zander muttered. "Harper, you like him. Heck, I like him. If he was gay I'd be all over him. It's okay to like a guy. I've been trying to get you to date for years. Being upset because he didn't call doesn't make you pathetic. It makes you human. I like you human."

Harper pursed her lips, conflicted. "You don't think it makes me weak?"

"No."

"How come I think it makes me look weak?"

"Because you're the most stubborn person I know," Zander answered. "You didn't want to open your heart to Jared from the beginning and now you're letting this lapse in judgment on his part reinforce the idea that he doesn't deserve you.

"Personally I don't think anyone is ever going to deserve you," he continued. "He's a good guy, though. I'm sure he didn't mean to send the wrong message when he didn't call."

Zander was always the king of the ego boost, and that was only one of the reasons Harper loved him. "Okay, let's say I believe you," she said. "What could his reasons be?"

Zander tilted his head to the side, considering. "Well, just off the top of my head, I'm guessing he thought you were going to call him and when you didn't he felt like an idiot and didn't call you because he was scared you would think *he* was weak."

"That's the stupidest thing I've ever heard."

"Why? That's exactly what you did," Zander challenged.

"Yes, but he's the one who left town," Harper pointed out. "It was his job to call me. His mother was hurt. Calling him would make me pathetic and invasive."

"Who says?"

"Everyone who has ever dated."

"Perhaps you and Jared should start your own traditions," Zander suggested. "Neither one of you are exactly pros at this. You said Jared admitted he wasn't big on dating before you and we both know how tragic your dating history is."

"Tragic being the operative word," Harper muttered.

Zander's expression softened. "Is that what's bothering you? Do you feel guilty dating Jared after Quinn? You know he would want you to be happy, right?"

"I don't feel guilty," Harper clarified. "I feel ... worried."

"About?"

"What if Jared only asked me out in the first place because he felt sorry for me?" Harper asked. "Poor, Harper. Her boyfriend died and she's been a spinster ever since. Maybe he only asked me out because he thought I would say no and he was hoping to earn points for being a good guy in the process."

"That makes absolutely no sense," Zander argued. "Jared is not the type of man who asks a woman out unless he wants to date her. In fact, Jared wasn't looking to date anyone until he met you. Then he couldn't stay away from you. That is the exact opposite of the nonsense you just spouted."

"But ...."

"No! Jared likes you. He came to our house. He saved our lives. That's not a man asking a woman out on a pity date. Get some perspective."

"Then why didn't he call?" Harper hated how whiny and needy she sounded. If anyone would understand her trepidation, though, it was Zander.

"Because he's just as nervous about all of this as you are," Zander answered, pushing a strand of Harper's shoulder-length blond hair away from her face. "You guys are a lot alike in some respects. He's terrified and you're freaking out every time I turn around. It's going to be a relief when you guys finally do it because I think it's going to take the edge off."

Harper was horrified. "What?"

"Oh, wipe that cute look off your face, Harper," Zander chided. "You need it. Whenever he looks at you it's obvious he needs it, too. It's going to happen."

"And what if I don't forgive him?"

Zander snorted. "I'm sorry." Instead of making things better, he made things worse when he bent over at the waist and guffawed loudly.

"Stop that," Harper hissed.

"I can't," Zander said, wiping a stray tear from his eye. "We both know you're going to forgive him. Now, I'm expecting you to make him jump through a few hoops before that happens. He deserves it, quite frankly.

"When he shows up with flowers and candy, you're not going to be able to stop yourself from kissing him senseless because he's got a certain ... pull ... where you're concerned," he continued. "Since he's put me through the wringer this week, I expect you to milk him for a special gift for me. I'm thinking ... um ... a nice dinner for both of us, cooked by him of course, would be a good start. Make sure he doesn't skimp on a bottle of wine. If it comes in a box, he's banished from the house forever."

Now it was Harper's turn to snort. "Just for the record, why would I invite you to a special dinner if I do forgive him?"

"Because I'm going to give him a hard time and it will be fun for you to watch because you won't be the bad guy in that scenario."

Despite herself, Harper felt a weight lift from her shoulders. "You really are my best friend."

"You're my best friend, too," Zander said, leaning over and briefly rubbing his nose against Harper's. "I ... ." The sound of pounding feet caught Zander's attention and he broke off, eyeing the teenage boy hurrying past him. "What's going on, Duncan?"

Duncan Cosgrove didn't slow his pace. "They found a body over at the park!"

Zander and Harper exchanged a look.

"Well, we have to check that out," Zander said. "Two bodies in three weeks? That's definitely got to be a record."

"**THIS** IS UNBELIEVABLE," Jared huffed, dumbfounded.

"You're telling me," Mel muttered, staring at the dead teenage boy on the ground near the merry-go-round at Whisper Cove's park. "I ... how could this happen?"

Jared lifted his eyes, momentarily surprised by Mel's words. Then it hit him: Mel knew everyone in Whisper Cove. He probably knew the victim, too. "Who is he?"

"His name is Derek Thompson. He's ... either seventeen or eighteen. Actually, I don't think he's eighteen yet."

"Good kid?"

"We don't really have bad kids here," Mel said. "Sure, we have some snots and mischief makers, but we haven't had a really bad kid since I joined the force. I ... his parents are in a euchre club with my wife and me. This is going to gut them."

"I'm really sorry," Jared said, meaning every word. "We have to get a handle on this, though."

"I thought that's what we were doing." Mel looked lost.

"We need to call the county coroner and we need to get this spot taped off," Jared said. "In fact ... why don't you do that? I'll take care of the preliminary examination on the body."

Mel looked relieved. "Thank you."

"I owe you," Jared said. "It's okay. I don't know him. It's rough because it's a kid, but it's not a kid I know. I can compartmentalize."

"I'll be better soon."

"Just get this area taped off," Jared instructed. "We both know we're going to be inundated with curiosity seekers in about five minutes. We need to keep them away from the body."

"I'm on it."

Jared watched Mel go, his heart going out to the man before turning his attention to the dead teenager. Derek Thompson was a handsome boy. He had dark brown hair and a chiseled jaw. Jared surveyed his body, taking mental notes. He looked like an athlete, strong shoulders and solid muscle tone belying hours spent working out.

His clothes were new. While they didn't look expensive, they weren't off brand. That suggested his parents had money, or that Derek had a job. Jared knew he had to find out which. Whisper Cove wasn't a rich community, but it wasn't poor either. Most of the denizens made decent livings.

Jared slapped a pair of rubber gloves into place and lifted Derek's hand so he could study his fingernails, searching for signs he fought off his assailant. He didn't have to look for a cause of death. The huge gash in the boy's forehead was definitely how he died. The question was: Did someone bash him in the head, or did he fall and hurt himself?

Jared scanned Derek's body. There were no obvious signs of a struggle other than the head wound. Perhaps they would get lucky and find the boy died from a fall. It was still a tragedy, but an accident was preferable to murder.

Jared focused on his task, zeroing in on possible clues. He wanted this to be quick so the coroner could take the body before a crowd gathered. It was time to focus.

"**DO** WE KNOW WHO IT IS?" Zander asked, peering over the police tape and frowning when he realized what he was looking at. "Uh-oh."

"Who is it?" Harper asked, Zander's tone worrying her. "Please tell me it's not someone we know. I ... ." She broke off when she saw Jared. "Oh, you've got to be kidding me."

Zander lowered his voice. "Do not make a scene here."

"Yes, because I love making a scene at the spot where a body is found," Harper deadpanned. "Does that even sound like something I would do?"

"Not generally," Zander conceded. "You're awfully worked up where Jared is concerned, though. I ... there's Uncle Mel."

As if sensing Zander and Harper's presence, Mel turned. He didn't appear surprised to see them. He trudged in their direction, his shoulders slouched.

"This doesn't look good," Harper murmured, her anger turning to concern.

"It doesn't," Zander agreed. "Hey, Uncle Mel. What's going on?"

"We have a body," Mel replied, rolling his neck until it cracked.

"Who?"

"I can't tell you that," Mel said. "We have to make notification ... to his parents."

Harper's heart sank. "It's child?"

"Teenager," Mel corrected hurriedly. "That's all I can tell you right now. We don't know how he died. Jared is going over his body now."

Harper and Zander exchanged a look. Mel seemed beaten down. That was the opposite of his usually gregarious self. This had to be bad.

"You can tell us," Zander prodded. "We'll keep it to ourselves. I promise."

"You know I can't do that," Mel said.

Movement out of the corner of her eye caught Harper's attention and she lifted her head, her stomach churning when she realized what she was looking at. "It's Derek Thompson, isn't it?"

Mel froze. "How do you know that?"

Harper pressed her lips together and remained silent.

"Is he a ... ghost?" Mel asked, glancing over his shoulder and focusing on the spot Harper stared. He was aware of Harper's reputation and the fact that she claimed to see ghosts. While he knew there was something special about the woman, he'd never been able to fully reconcile the idea of her talking to ghosts. Now he wasn't so sure. The body was too far away for her to make identification and she was staring intently at the tree line behind the merry-go-round. "Can you see him?"

"Yes."

"Oh, no," Zander said, wrapping an arm around Harper's shoulders. He glanced around, but more and more people from town were joining the fray. "You can't try to talk to him now, Harp. There are too many people."

"I know." Harper felt as if her heart was breaking. "This is awful."

"It's about to get worse," Zander muttered, frowning as Jared moved up behind Mel.

"I'm done," Jared said. "The coroner can take him right away. I ... ." Jared broke off when he saw Harper. "Hi."

Harper opened her mouth to answer but no sound would come out. Instead of standing there looking like an idiot, she turned on her heel and stomped away.

Jared turned to Zander. "Are you ticked off, too?"

"You're a very bad man," Zander hissed. "You'd better bring gifts and be prepared to beg when you show up. Now, if you'll excuse me, I have to make sure she doesn't damage anyone's property on the walk back to the office. This is so not good."

"Wait," Mel whispered. "What about the ghost?"

Zander shrugged. "We can't do anything with all these people around," he said. "We'll try to come back later. I'll tell you if we find something."

FIVE

"S on of a ... ." Jared watched Harper hurry away, frustrated.

"That went well," Mel deadpanned, regaining a modicum of swagger even though he was still pale and grim.

"Women are crazy," Jared muttered.

"Do you honestly blame her for being upset?"

Jared searched his heart. "No. I do blame her for walking away from a crime scene when she knows I can't leave and follow her. Zander isn't exactly helping matters."

Mel snorted. "He told you what you wanted to hear. You just weren't listening."

"What did he tell me?"

"He told you to be prepared to beg and bring gifts," Mel pointed out. "That means he knows she's going to forgive you. I'd take that as a good sign. No one knows Harper better than Zander."

"That's one of the things that drives me crazy," Jared admitted. "No matter how well I get to know her, he's going to know her better."

"You're looking at it from the wrong perspective," Mel said. "You're looking at Zander as a man who knows your potential woman better than you do. If Zander was a woman, would it bother you as much?"

Jared mulled the question. "No."

"Why not?"

"Because women are chatty and talk about everything – including their feelings – to death," Jared responded.

"Harper has never really had any female friends," Mel said. "Zander is her best friend. They're never going to be romantically involved. Just think of Zander as a woman."

"Isn't that stereotypical and offensive?"

Mel shrugged. "Harper tells him he complains like a woman all of the time," he said. "I don't think he takes it personally. Now, if you wear socks and sandals together, that he takes personally."

Despite himself, Jared smirked. "I wish I could go after her."

"I wish you could, too," Mel said. "You can't, though. We have to find out what happened to Derek. If it wasn't an accident … ."

"Then we have a murderer loose," Jared finished, inclining his chin in the direction of the nearby parking lot. "Here comes the medical examiner."

"Good. Hopefully he can give us some information. We're not going to be able to hold off for very long without informing Kim and Scott that their son is dead."

Jared pressed his lips together, thoughtful. "I can do that for you," he said finally.

"I appreciate it," Mel said. "This isn't a duty I can push off on someone else, though. They're my friends. I owe them the respect to be the one to tell them."

"**THIS** COULD HONESTLY GO EITHER WAY." Macomb County's chief medical examiner Tom Pfeiffer studied Derek's head wound. "The blow was hard enough that someone could've inflicted it on him, or he could've fallen and accidentally did it to himself."

Jared glanced around. "If he fell, what did he fall on?"

Tom shrugged. "Do you notice any blood on the merry-go-round anywhere?"

Jared shook his head. "I looked. It's old. A lot of it is rusty. I didn't see anything. That doesn't mean there's nothing there."

"I can't really give you serious answers until I do a full autopsy and it might not be completed until tomorrow," Tom said. "I'll do my best to get it in today, but we need to put a rush on toxicology results because they could have an impact here. I just ... I can't promise you anything."

"Do your best," Mel instructed. "Get him out of here, though. Word is starting to spread. Make sure he's covered so no one can catch sight of him. We need to make notification to the parents."

"Good luck," Tom said. "I don't envy what's in front of you."

"That's funny," Mel said. "I would say the same thing to you."

Jared and Mel watched Tom load up Derek's body and instructed two uniformed police officers to watch the scene and make sure no one breached it. Then they headed toward the Thompson house with heavy hearts and grim determination. Jared drove while Mel navigated, the younger detective watching his new partner become more and more antsy as they grew closer to their destination.

"I can do this without you," Jared offered, his voice low.

"No, you can't."

Since he'd met Mel, Jared had never seen the older man lose his nerve. He was almost always singularly gregarious and effusive. Now he appeared to be shrinking in the passenger seat of the car.

"I think you're a brave man," Jared said as he parked in front of the Thompson's brick colonial. "I'll help you however I can."

Mel shot Jared a half-hearted smile. "I think you're a brave man," he said. "Only someone with true courage would date Harper and Zander."

"I'm not dating Zander."

Mel snorted. "You are. You just don't know it yet."

Jared and Mel pulled themselves together for the long walk up the short driveway. Jared knocked, patting Mel's back before straightening his shoulders and gracing the middle-aged woman who answered the door with a solemn look.

"Hi, Kim," Mel said, shifting uncomfortable.

Kim Thompson was a pretty woman. In her younger years she probably would've qualified as "beautiful" on almost every scale. She was still a looker, but as her eyes met Mel's and realization started to dawn it was almost as if she aged twenty years in front of Jared's eyes. "I ... what are you doing here, Mel?"

"Can we come in?"

Kim bit her lip. Jared didn't know the woman – he'd never laid eyes on her until today – and yet he could read every stray thought as it flitted through her mind. She wanted to go back in time. She wanted to pick a time before she answered the door. She wanted to wake up in her own bed and start the day over again. She hadn't heard the worst news she was ever going to hear yet, but she was already rationalizing some way out of her predicament.

"Ma'am, can we come inside?" Jared asked, his tone gentle.

Kim pushed open the door, taking a step back and ushering Mel and Jared inside. "I ... ."

"What's going on?" Scott Thompson appeared in the hallway, a newspaper in his hand. "Hey, Mel. Are you here for me to school you in euchre again?" Unlike his wife Scott hadn't come to an awful conclusion at the sight of his friend. Jared wished him a few more seconds of jocularity before reality set in.

"We need to talk, Scott," Mel said, his voice even. Jared marveled at his partner's ability to hold himself together even though he was sure Mel wanted to fall apart with his friends.

"What's wrong?" Scott asked, reaching for Kim's shaking hand. It was as if he already knew the answer.

"Maybe you should sit down," Mel suggested.

"Tell me."

"We found Derek about two hours ago," Mel said, opting to rip the Band-Aid off rather than watch his friends suffer. "He was near the merry-go-round at the town park. There's no other way to tell you this so ... I'm sorry. He's dead."

"No!" Kim's wail wasn't something Jared would soon forget. He was stoic as he watched the woman crumple, her husband struggling to hold her steady, but inside his heart hurt. How were parents supposed to survive the loss of their child?

"I DON'T UNDERSTAND any of this," Scott said, pacing the living room as Kim curled up in a chair and cried. She hadn't said a word since Mel told her the bad news, and Jared was legitimately worried about how pale she was. "We didn't even know he was out of the house. I … how is that possible?"

"He's a teenager, Scott," Mel said, choosing his words carefully. "You don't watch teenagers twenty-four hours a day. It can't be done."

"But … how long has he been dead?"

"The medical examiner is taking him back to do a full autopsy," Mel replied. "We're not sure yet. The best guess is that he died between midnight and two this morning. We'll have more information when the autopsy is finished."

Kim stifled a sob and buried her face in her hands. The idea of her child being cut open was almost too much to bear. Instead of going to her and offering comfort, though, Scott maintained his distance. They were a couple, but they were dealing with their tragedy in different ways. Kim was ready to wallow and disappear. Scott wanted answers and was fueled by anger. Eventually they would meet in the middle. For now, though, they were on separate paths.

"Who are your suspects?" Scott pressed. "Who killed my son?"

Jared and Mel exchanged a wary look.

"We don't know if it was murder yet," Jared cautioned. "The medical examiner says it's too early to tell."

"If it wasn't murder, what was it? A seventeen-year-old boy doesn't just drop dead from natural causes!"

Jared rubbed the back of his neck. "He had a wound on his head," he explained. "The problem is, he could've been struck – which would mean we're looking for a killer – or he could've stumbled and hit his own head. He was very close to the merry-go-round. We just don't know yet."

"Stumble? Derek is an athlete. He doesn't stumble."

"Scott, I know this is a terrible time, but you need to calm down," Mel instructed. "I do not want to cast aspersions on Derek because he was a good kid, but we don't know if he was out there drinking with other kids or ... ."

"Derek didn't drink!" Kim snapped. "He was a good boy."

"I'm not saying he wasn't a good boy," Mel countered. "Of course he was a good boy. Even good boys party at that age. Don't you remember what it was like when you were the same age? I like to consider myself a relatively good man, but I liked to party back then, too. I seem to remember you two partying along with me when we were in high school."

Kim bit her lip, conflicted.

"Even if Derek was out partying, he was still a good boy," Mel added. "Until we know exactly how he died, though, we're stuck."

"So you're not going to do anything?" Scott challenged.

"Of course we're going to do something," Mel answered. "We're going to find out if anyone else was out there last night. We're going to wait for the medical examiner's report. We need facts to move forward. We're going to get those facts."

"You make sure you do," Scott said. "I want whoever killed my boy to pay!"

THAT WAS ... SURREAL," Jared said an hour later, leaning back in the driver's seat of the patrol car and casting a sidelong look in Mel's direction. "How are you feeling?"

"Like I've been run over by a train."

"I don't blame you," Jared said. "That was rough."

"It was almost as if Scott was accusing me of not caring about Derek," Mel said. "I don't understand how he could think that. I loved the boy, too."

"When people are grieving they say and do things they wouldn't normally say or do," Jared said. "Scott is so angry at losing his son he needs someone to blame. You're the only target right now because he doesn't know me well enough to accuse me of anything.

"I hate to say it, but you want him blaming you right now, because when things shift and he starts blaming himself … well … then things are really going to get rough," he said.

Mel frowned. "Why would he blame himself?"

"You heard him," Jared replied. "He didn't know his son was even out last night. They thought Derek was upstairs sleeping the whole night. He wasn't. He was out. They don't want to think he might've been doing something they wouldn't approve of so they'd rather blame you. That will change."

"I guess," Mel said, pressing the heel of his hand against his forehead. "We have a lot of things to look at. I wouldn't be surprised if the kids were out in that park drinking last night. Those woods provide natural cover, and the park is far enough away from the downtown that most people can't see what's going on from the road."

"Did you guys drink there when you were younger?"

Mel nodded. "It's always been a teenage party spot," he said. "If you walk back into those woods about a half a mile out there's even a slow-moving river. We used to party out there, too.

"Heck, when Zander and Harper were teenagers I busted them partying out there and Zander declared me the world's biggest hypocrite when his mother told him about how I used to party out there," he continued.

Jared smirked. "I'll bet those two were cute when they were drunk as teenagers."

"Zander was drunk that night as I recall," Mel countered. "Harper wasn't. She never let herself drink too much."

"How come?"

"She always had trouble letting go," Mel answered. "I think … I think seeing the things she sees wears on her. If she's not careful, she might have a tendency to drink too much to dull her senses. I think she's always worried about stuff like that."

"I never thought of that," Jared admitted.

"Speaking of Harper, someone needs to go and talk to her," Mel said pointedly.

"I'll handle my problems with Harper," Jared said. "I don't think my romantic issues take precedence over a possible murder investigation."

Mel chuckled. "That's not what I was talking about," he said. "Before you interrupted us, Harper knew who the victim was. She was staring at the tree line behind Derek's body. The only way she could know who was dead is if she saw Derek's ghost."

"I thought you couldn't decide if Harper really saw ghosts?" Jared pressed.

"How else did she know who died? She couldn't see who was on the ground. The merry-go-round was in the way. Besides, I thought you believed her?"

"I *do* believe her," Jared said. "I just don't want to grovel."

"Well, you're going to have to get over it," Mel said. "We need her to try and talk to Derek's ghost. Right now he's the only one who knows what happened in that park last night."

"I guess that means I need to buy some flowers."

"Don't forget the candy," Mel instructed. "You need to make sure you cover all of your bases."

"Thanks for the tip."

"Don't mention it," Mel said. "While you're doing that, I'm going to go and see if I can find any of the kids who usually hang out at the park. Someone has to have seen something."

"For now, that's all we can do," Jared agreed. "Just for curiosity's sake, how do I look?"

Mel scowled. "I don't care how you look. I'm not going to go out with you."

"Yes, but would you forgive me if you were a woman?"

"Son, you're starting to freak me out," Mel said. "There's such a thing as being too close."

Jared sighed. "I'd settle for being just close enough to touch her right now."

"You've got it bad."

"What was your first clue?"

"That morose look on your face when she stormed off," Mel replied, not missing a beat. "Now, come on. I need to start asking questions and you need to go and beg a certain blonde for forgiveness. I hate to say it, but she's looking to be our best shot at getting ahead on this one."

"You never told me how I look," Jared prodded.

"You're a hunk of burning love."

Jared made a face. "I'm not sure that's a compliment."

SIX

"Well, I think I handled that well," Harper announced, striding into the GHI office and dramatically throwing herself in her desk chair. They'd taken the roundabout way back – stopping in the local diner for lunch and a gossip session to see if anyone knew anything about the hoopla at the park – and now they could finally talk about the real afternoon excitement. "That looked cool, right?"

"That looked way cool," Zander agreed, offering her an enthusiastic thumbs-up. "When you twirled, your hair flew at just the right level. You added that little twitch into your step, too. That was impressive. He had no idea what happened to him."

"Who had no idea what happened to him?" Molly asked, her fork halfway to her mouth as she ate a salad at the corner table. "I thought you guys were getting ice cream and making up. How did you manage to find drama between here and the ice cream shop?"

"We *did* make up," Zander announced. "We're back to being BFFs and acting as a united front. That's why we're being extremely dramatic in tandem instead of using it as a weapon against each other."

"I don't think we're being *that* dramatic," Harper countered.

"Yes, because that little twirl you did wasn't straight out of *General*

Hospital," Zander countered. "We were dramatic, Harp. It's a good thing in this case."

"Why are you being dramatic?" Eric asked, wiping his hands on a napkin as he finished his sandwich in the spot across from Molly. "Why do I think we're missing huge pieces of the story?"

"Because they haven't told a story yet," Molly supplied, causing Eric to roll his eyes.

"Well, for starters, there was a body in the park," Zander said, launching into his tale. "We got there after the police, but the victim is Derek Thompson. He's a local teenager and Harper saw his ghost. It's too soon to tell if he was murdered or accidentally died, though, so we're going to have to wait until Harper can talk to the ghost to find out more information on that."

"Derek Thompson," Molly mused. "That name sounds familiar for some reason."

"He's the son of Scott and Kim Thompson," Zander explained. "They're euchre buddies with Uncle Mel. You met them at that barbecue he had last fall."

"Oh, no," Molly said, her excitement diminishing. "I remember them. They seemed sweet … and the mother couldn't stop bragging about her son. That's horrible."

"It is," Zander agreed.

"I don't understand how that leads to you and Harper being dramatic," Eric prodded. "Was there a scene at the … um … scene?"

Molly smirked at the play on words, a momentary flash of adoration flitting across her face before she sobered.

"Jared is back in town," Zander announced. "He took one look at Harper and said 'hi' like an imbecile, and then she did this really awesome turnaround and flounced away. The only thing that would've made it better is if her hair was long enough to whip him in the face."

Eric frowned. "Jared is back? I hope you told him where to stick it, Harper. He doesn't deserve you after what he did."

"I just told you she didn't speak to him," Zander replied, narrowing his eyes. "She left him speechless. It was the perfect reintroduction."

"I like Jared," Molly said. "He's really handsome and sweet. I think he has a reason for not calling. I don't think we should hate him until we know he's a douchebag."

"I already know he's a douchebag," Eric said. " Only a douchebag wouldn't bother to call for ten days."

The sound of someone knocking on the front door of the office caused everyone to turn, finding Jared standing in the open doorway Harper and Zander forgot to close as they returned. "Is the office still open for douchebags?" Jared asked, tightening his grip on the bouquet of roses he held.

Eric's cheeks colored as Jared fixed him with a challenging look. "I don't think we were expecting you," Eric said, recovering quickly. "If you need to meet with someone, I guess I can clear some time."

Jared rolled his eyes until they landed on Harper. "I'm here to see her."

"I don't think she wants to see you," Eric said.

"Shh," Zander commanded, moving closer to Jared and lifting the bouquet so he could study it. "This is an interesting choice. What made you go with purple roses?"

"I didn't like the red ones because they looked like they were about to die," Jared replied, never moving his eyes from Harper's face. "They had pink ones, but I was told those mean friendship and I'm not feeling very friendly."

"Good choice," Zander said. "Harper's not a fan of pink unless it's really bright and on shoes. What's in that box you're carrying?" Zander zeroed in on Jared's other hand, where he clutched a velvet heart-shaped box.

Jared handed the candy over. "It's caramel. Make sure you save some of that for Harper."

"No promises," Zander said, tearing open the box. "Okay, Harp, I approve of his gifts. You may go outside and speak to him, but don't forget what I told you about the proper bribe for me when you're out there."

Jared wrenched his eyes away from Harper and watched Zander

pop a chocolate heart into his mouth. "Why am I bribing you? I'm here to bribe her."

"I'm the way to her heart."

"Whatever," Jared muttered, turning back to Harper. "Can we talk outside?"

"I don't think that's a good idea," Eric answered for Harper, causing her to make a face. "She's decided that you're out of her life."

"No one asked you," Jared shot back. "I'm here to talk to Harper and I'm not leaving until I do. Now, if I have to do it in front of all of you, I will. It's going to be unpleasant, though, and if any of you say one thing I don't like I'm going to arrest you."

"On what charge?" Zander challenged.

"Annoying me," Jared replied, not missing a beat.

Harper sighed. "Fine. We can go outside to talk. I don't think this is going to end how you think it's going to end, though."

"Way to be strong, Harp," Zander said. "Do not give in until he cooks us both dinner and buys an expensive bottle of wine to make up for his gross negligence in the boyfriend department."

Harper's cheeks colored as she got to her feet, causing her to avert her eyes. "He wasn't my boyfriend."

Jared studied her a moment, frustrated. He didn't know what annoyed him more: having to grovel in front of people, having to pretend he didn't notice the way Eric's predatory eyes moved up and down Harper's lithe body, or the way Harper refused to refer to him as her boyfriend. Actually, all three of those things bothered him.

"No, I *am* her boyfriend," Jared said, taking himself by surprise with his fortitude. "We're just having a ... misunderstanding."

Harper scowled and moved toward the front door, grumbling as she walked. "Misunderstanding my ass," she muttered. "Ten days without one call is not a misunderstanding. A misunderstanding is accidentally forgetting to call at lunchtime when you say you're going to and not remembering until it's almost time for dinner. It's not forgetting a person existed for ten days straight."

Jared followed her, the inclination to shake her and kiss her warring for supremacy. He'd almost forgotten how cute she was. He wouldn't make that mistake again. He cast a look over his shoulder and focused on Zander as he reached to shut the door behind them. "I'll be taking her home after this," he said. "Whatever dinner thing you have planned, I'll handle when this Derek Thompson case is solved."

"I want steak and red-skinned potatoes."

"Fine," Jared said. "You'd better be on my side when she starts complaining about me. I have a feeling this isn't going to be over as fast as I would like."

"I'm always on your side," Zander replied.

"Don't eat all of that candy," Jared warned. "It was expensive and she should get at least once piece."

"Oh, she's been mainlining candy since you forgot she existed," Zander said. "I'm sure she'll survive."

Jared scowled and slammed the office door as he left, cringing when Harper swiveled and placed her hands on her hips.

"What do you want?"

Jared knew he was supposed to be cowering in fear and begging, but there was something so appealing about Harper and her simple blue jeans and T-shirt that he was momentarily lost in thought. "What?"

"God, you forgot about me when you were standing across from me," Harper snapped, shaking her head.

"I did not forget about you," Jared argued. "I ... made a mistake."

"Oh, wow, thanks for the news flash," Harper deadpanned. "I'll alert the media."

Jared ran his tongue over his teeth. "You have a right to be angry."

"Thank you for your permission."

Jared rubbed his hand over the top of his hair, completely dumbfounded how to handle this situation. Mel was right when he said he had no idea what he was doing. Jared was at a loss. He knew he wanted to make things better. He just didn't know how.

For lack of anything better to do, Jared extended the flowers so Harper could take them. "I know you're supposed to get red in a situation like this, but I didn't like the look of the red ones," he said. "The purple reminded me of you for some reason."

Harper took the flowers, her eyes widening as she looked them over. "You must have spent a fortune on these."

"I had no idea flowers were so expensive. You're the first person I've ever bought them for."

"How did you know purple was my favorite color? Did Zander tell you?" Harper asked, her blue eyes sharp as they studied his face.

"No. I honestly ... for some reason those were the ones I liked so I went with my gut," Jared replied. "I ... ." He broke off, conflicted.

Harper waited.

"I'm sorry," Jared said, gritting the words out. "I didn't mean to hurt you."

Harper's cheeks flooded, burning as shame washed over her. "You didn't hurt me. I ... that's ridiculous. Who said you hurt me? I didn't say that."

Jared pursed his lips. "It's obvious I hurt you," he said. "I didn't mean to. I ... don't have an excuse except I wanted you to call me. When you didn't, I felt like an idiot and it was too late to call you without looking like an ass. I figured we would just catch up when I got back."

"Huh. Well ... I guess we're caught up," Harper said, making to move back into the office. "Have a nice day."

"Don't walk away from me," Jared ordered, softening his voice when he caught sight of the murderous look on her face. "I really am sorry. This is the last thing I wanted."

"What did you want?"

"I wanted a chance to go on a date with you before I got called out of town and screwed everything up."

Jared's answer was honest and earnest, and despite her best intentions, Harper felt her resolve melting. "It doesn't matter."

"It *does* matter."

"No, it doesn't," Harper argued. "I thought ... it doesn't matter what I thought." She regrouped. "I'm glad your mother is doing better.

I'm sorry you had to come home to a murder. I ... thank you for the flowers."

Jared knit his eyebrows together. "Is that it?"

"That's it. You may go."

"Not bloody likely." Jared grabbed the front of Harper's shirt, taking her by surprise, and planted a scorching kiss on her lips.

She thought about fighting him, but her body wouldn't let her. She leaned into the kiss, causing him to pull her flush against his chest. Neither one of them made a move to come up for air, instead losing themselves in each other and ten days of building anticipation.

"OH, MAN!" Eric made a disgusted sound in the back of his throat. "I can't believe she fell for flowers and chocolate."

"I told you," Zander said, smirking as he popped another caramel heart into his mouth. "They're an attractive couple. I can't wait to see him with his shirt off."

Molly giggled, stepping between Eric and Zander and watching Harper and Jared make out on the sidewalk in front of the office. "Do you think they're officially back on?"

Zander shook his head. "I've got twenty bucks that says Jared assumes everything is peachy and Harper punishes him for another twenty-four hours."

Eric looked hopeful. "Maybe she'll realize he's a bad kisser and dump him right now."

Molly rolled her eyes. "He doesn't look like a bad kisser."

"He's not a bad kisser," Zander said. "Harper told me she saw stars when he finally kissed her."

"Ugh." Eric looked as if he wanted to throw up.

"They're cute," Zander said, smiling fondly at his best friend. "Too bad it's going to be at least one more day of drama before they're officially lovey-dovey again."

"I think it's going to be fun," Molly said. "Harper deserves to have her heart flip. She's waited a long time for someone like Jared to come along."

"I just hope he cooks me a good dinner," Zander said. "The only way I'm officially getting back on his side is if he wows me with a delicious steak."

"This sucks," Eric muttered.

"Get over it," Zander instructed. "They fit together. I like him. He makes her smile. She deserves everything he's going to bring to her life."

"What if he upsets her again?" Eric protested.

"That's life," Zander replied, nonplussed. "Nothing is ever perfect. He is, however, perfect for my Harp. He just needs to learn to buy more than one box of chocolate next time he screws up. Harper is going to be sad she missed this round."

SEVEN

"I don't think I agreed to this." Harper glanced around the park, frowning as the setting sun caused her to narrow her eyes. "How did this even happen?"

Jared shrugged as he ushered her down the slight embankment and toward the taped-off area where Derek Thompson's body was discovered. "I think I managed to sneak the request in between kisses."

Harper scowled. "You don't play fair."

"What's that saying about everything being fair in love and war?" Jared challenged.

"Which one is this?" Harper knew she was putting him on the spot, and she relished her power as he shifted uncomfortably.

"I think it might be too soon to tell," Jared replied smoothly, although his blue eyes took on a far-off look. "I missed you, Harper."

His voice was so soft when he said the words Harper wasn't sure she didn't imagine them. She glanced at him. "Did you just say ... ?" She didn't want to ask the question in case it made her look needy – or ridiculous if she imagined it – so she snapped her mouth shut.

"I said that I missed you," Jared repeated, holding her gaze. "If you think I'm embarrassed to say it, then you don't know me. I'm not embarrassed ... and I did miss you."

Harper frowned. "You have a funny way of showing it."

"I know."

Harper shook her head, dislodging the warm and fuzzy feelings rolling around inside of her. "I'm still mad at you."

"Duly noted," Jared said, pressing his hand to the small of her back and urging her forward. "I'm not here to get you to forgive me."

"Then why are we here?" Harper asked, scanning the area.

"Mel said you saw Derek Thompson's ghost earlier," Jared replied, keeping his voice low. "I was hoping you would be able to talk to him and find out what happened. If a young man's death gets in the way of your anger ... well ... I guess I can take you home."

"Oh, well, that's playing fair," Harper said, sarcasm practically dripping from her tongue.

"I'm not here to play fair," Jared whispered, pressing his mouth close to Harper's ear and enjoying the way she involuntarily shivered. It took him a minute to get his bearings, the feeling of her warm body momentarily giving him ideas, but the memory of Kim's anguished face pulled him back to reality. Now wasn't the time to play games. He forced himself to take a step back. "Can you see Derek?"

Harper shot Jared a dirty look. "You did that on purpose."

"What?"

"You know what," Harper snapped, although she turned her attention to the quiet park. "He was over here earlier," she said, picking her way to a spot close to the tree line.

"What was he doing?" Jared asked, focusing on the seriousness of the case.

"He was just standing here and watching everyone group around his body," Harper answered. "He looked ... confused."

"Is that normal?" Jared asked, leaning over to study the ground where Harper pointed. "I mean ... do ghosts realize what has happened to them?"

"Most of them understand that they're not still alive," Harper replied. "A lot of them think they're trapped in a dream. Others are ... confused ... by their new reality."

"So you're basically saying you have no idea what Derek is feeling," Jared surmised.

Harper scowled. "You're an ass."

"That wasn't a dig," Jared argued. "You can take it however you want, but it was not a dig. I know you're angry with me for not calling …."

Harper crossed her arms over her chest. "I don't care about you not calling. Why would I? It's not like we made some sort of … promise to one another before you left. We shared one kiss. You said maybe we would go out on a date. I'm not the sort of woman who gets pathetic and clingy so …."

Jared tugged on his ear as he studied her. She was a mystery. He couldn't wrap his head around what she was feeling from one moment to the next. "Are you saying you don't want to date me?"

"No. Yes. No. I … what was the question?" Harper was beyond flustered.

Jared smirked. She was just as worked up as he was. "Do you know what I think?"

"That you wish you'd never bought me flowers?"

Jared shook his head. "I think you're amped up," he said. "I think you thought I was going to call and when I didn't you couldn't help feeling hurt. Don't bother arguing with me. There's nothing embarrassing about that.

"I should have called you," he continued. "The truth is … I was embarrassed myself. I didn't want to look needy. The first thought that occurred to me once I checked on my mother was calling you. Do you know what I told myself?"

Harper bit her lip and shook her head.

"I told myself you and Zander would make fun of me for calling you so soon," Jared explained. "So I didn't call. I had dinner alone in front of the television after my mother went to sleep. I sat there and wondered what you were doing. I pictured you and Zander getting in your pajamas and watching some … chick flick or something. Don't ever tell him I said that, by the way. He'll accuse me of stereotyping him and that's the last thing I want because I'm going to need him on my side.

"So then I woke up the next morning and I was going to call you before I even got out of bed," he continued. "I worried it was too early, so I had breakfast. Then I told myself you were probably working a job and I would call you after dinner. I didn't do that, though, because then I started wondering why you hadn't called me.

"I spent the next three hours obsessing about what you were doing and why you hadn't called me," Jared said. "By the time I went to bed I was ticked off because you hadn't bothered to check in and see how my mother was doing. When I woke up the next morning the whole thing started all over again. The truth is ... well ... I didn't call you because I flipped myself out. Are you happy?"

Despite herself, Harper couldn't help the feeling of warmth that rolled over her. "I am. Thank you."

Jared scowled. "Is that it? Does that mean we've made up?"

Harper shook her head, her blond hair glinting as the descending sun bounced off it. "I'm not ready to forgive you yet. You really hurt my feelings."

"You don't want to take any responsibility for this?"

"It wasn't my place to call you," Harper replied. "Your mother was injured and sick. I would never call in case you were in the hospital and I accidentally woke her ... or if you were talking to a doctor and I interrupted. It was your place to call."

"And this is simply because my mother was sick and not some twisted gender roles thing, right?"

Harper narrowed her eyes into dangerous blue slits. "What are you saying? Are you saying I'm a needy chick who expects you to do all the work in this relationship?"

"Hah!" Jared hopped up and down, pointing. "You just called it a relationship. From now on, when someone calls me your boyfriend, that means you have to admit I'm your boyfriend."

"No way," Harper protested. "A boyfriend calls."

"I've apologized for not calling," Jared growled. "I regret it. If I could go back in time ... you know what? If I could go back in time I would get my mother a different rug so she wouldn't slip and fall and hurt herself. That way we could've gone out on a real date and not been separated for ten days. That's what I would've done."

"Oh, well … ." Harper flapped her hands. "It's hard to stay angry with you when you're so hot and sweet. Stop it!"

Jared chuckled. "Fine. If you want to stay angry, stay angry." He reached out and grabbed Harper's hand, linking their fingers. "I'm not going to stay angry, so good luck pretending you're mad at me. I'm going to keep my mouth shut and watch you work. I'll be right here … holding your hand."

"That won't make this difficult or anything," Harper huffed.

Jared didn't respond, instead focusing on the high ridges of her cheekbones as they searched the area. Her face was beautiful, her eyes bright and inquisitive. He liked watching her work, even if she was less than thrilled with the manner in which he watched her. He couldn't help but be fascinated by every little thing she did. He realized Mel was right on several fronts. He was already a goner where she was concerned.

"Did you hear me?"

"Huh?" Jared shifted his attention to Harper. "What?"

"Why do you keep forgetting me?" Harper complained.

"I didn't forget you. I was thinking."

"About what?" Harper asked, rolling her neck until it cracked.

"I was thinking you're probably the most beautiful woman I've seen in real life," Jared responded, guileless.

"I … um … oh … well … ." Harper was at a loss for words. That just made her more adorable in Jared's book.

"You two are just too cute for school."

Harper jumped at the new voice, clutching Jared's hand and causing him to crash back to reality. She swiveled, fixing Derek Thompson with a surprised look. "Derek."

"He's here?" Jared asked, moving closer to her.

Harper nodded. "Derek, do you know who I am?"

"You're the dippy blond chick who thinks she talks to ghosts and hangs around with Mel's gay nephew," Derek replied, causing Harper to frown.

"You know you're dead, right?" Harper asked. "If I'm so dippy, how come I'm talking to you?"

Jared fought the mad urge to laugh as he listened to her hold a conversation with thin air. In his head he knew she was talking to someone, but it bothered him that he couldn't share the experience with her.

Derek shrugged. "I guess that's a pretty good question," he said, glancing around. "Where did everyone go?"

"Everyone who?" Harper asked. "Were you here with other people?"

"When?"

Harper bit her tongue to keep from lashing out. It wasn't Derek's fault that he was confused. "Let's take it from the top," she suggested. "What's the last thing you remember?"

"You were about to start groping Mel's new partner in the park when you were supposed to be finding me," Derek replied, not missing a beat.

"We were not about to start groping one another!"

This time Jared couldn't swallow his chuckle in time to keep it from escaping. Harper refused to acknowledge him, or the surreal nature of the situation.

"Oh, puh-leez," Derek intoned. "I'm not an idiot. You two were two seconds from smooching."

"Whatever," Harper muttered. "We weren't going to smooch."

"We already did that for ten minutes on the street," Jared added. Even though he couldn't see Derek he felt like being involved in the conversation.

"Thanks for that," Harper said dryly.

"You're welcome."

Harper inhaled deeply, calming herself. They were there on a mission and she couldn't lose track of that. "Do you know what happened to you last night, Derek?"

"I ... ." Derek cocked his head to the side, furrowing his brow as he racked his brain. "I can't remember much of anything," he admitted after a few seconds. "It's like my head is mush." He chuckled harshly at his own joke. "Technically I guess my head did end up being mush, didn't it?"

"Do you remember leaving your house last night? Your parents didn't know you were out. Did you sneak out?"

"I didn't have to sneak out," Derek replied. "My parents didn't keep tabs on me. My dad was watching television when I left and Mom was in bed reading a book."

"Did you go straight to the park?"

"I ... don't know."

"What do you remember?"

"I just said I don't know! Are you deaf?"

Derek was frustrated and shaken. Harper didn't blame him. She held her hands up in a placating manner. "It's okay, Derek. This is all still new to you. Maybe if you take some time and think about things you'll remember what happened."

"Yeah, and then everything will be great," Derek said, his eyes flashing. "You know what? I was right from the start. You are dippy."

"I didn't say things would be great," Harper clarified. "I just said ...
."

Derek cut her off. "I'm out of here. I don't want to hang around with the strange chick who can talk to ghosts."

"Derek!" He was already gone.

"What happened?" Jared asked.

"I forgot how much I hated teenagers," Harper lamented.

"That bad, huh?"

"He's not coming back tonight," Harper said. "He's petulant, pouty, and has attitude."

Jared reached over and gathered her hand again, squeezing it. "You tried."

"I don't think that's enough," Harper admitted. "He's here for a reason. If he died by accident, he probably would've already passed over on his own. That means something happened to him."

"You think he was murdered, don't you?"

"I don't know what else to think."

Jared lifted Harper's hand and pressed a kiss to her palm. "Come on. I'll take you home. You need another night to be mad at me so we can make up completely tomorrow. The sooner you go to sleep, the sooner we'll be happy again."

Harper arched a challenging eyebrow. "You're awfully sure of yourself."

"Just wait until tomorrow," Jared said, his smile wolfish. "You're going to be awfully sure of me, too."

"Oh, finally, something to look forward to." Harper reluctantly let Jared lead her back toward his vehicle, casting one more glance over her shoulder in the hope she would see Derek. He wasn't there, though.

"I'm going to give you so many things to look forward to you're going to lose count," Jared promised.

"Like what?"

"I'm going to make a list before I go to bed."

"Well, I do like a planner," Harper teased, giving in to the banter. "If I do decide to forgive you tomorrow, you need to cook a huge dinner for Zander. He wants steak and wine that doesn't come from a box."

"I think I can handle that."

EIGHT

"So the ghost couldn't tell you anything?" Eric asked Harper the next morning, keeping close to her as she walked up a gravel driveway in the direction of a riverfront cabin. "That sucks."

Harper forced a smile. Eric wasn't her first choice of scouting partners – mostly because his crush was becoming increasingly distracting and she was desperate to find a way to force him to look elsewhere for a love interest without hurting his feelings – but Zander was stuck in the office doing spreadsheets and she was still leery about taking Molly out on too many assignments. "He seemed upset," she explained. "I'm hoping he'll come around when he settles into his new reality a little more. Unfortunately, if he doesn't want help, I can't force him to show up and talk to me."

"You'd think he'd want to talk to you," Eric said. "You're the only one around who he can talk to. That pretty much makes you his best friend right now. Or ... at least it should."

"He's at that age where you think you know everything and the realization that you actually know nothing is a blow."

"I guess. You'd still think he would be nicer to his best shot of moving on to a better place," Eric said. "So, um ... how did things go with Jared?"

Harper internally cringed at the question. "They were fine."

"Fine?"

"Fine," Harper repeated. She cleared her throat and decided to change the subject before she had to listen to another diatribe about Jared being a douchebag. "Eric, what do you think about Molly?"

Eric stiffened. "What do you mean?"

Harper realized the reason behind the shift in his demeanor right away. "I'm not going to pressure you to date her," she said, her voice soft. "I think Zander is doing that enough for everybody. I want to know what you think about how she's been acting since her ordeal."

"Oh," Eric said, exhaling heavily. "I don't know what to think about that." He followed Harper as she circled to the side of the cottage. "What are we doing here again?"

"The cottage is up for sale and it's a great parcel," Harper replied. "Unfortunately strange things keep happening and the real estate agent is convinced it's haunted. I'm trying to ascertain if that's true before we quote her a price on clearing it."

"Do you think she's making it up?"

"I think sometimes people see things that aren't there," Harper replied. "I want to make sure that something is really haunting this place before we talk about a plan of action. If there is something here, we should be able to find it pretty quickly. It's a small place – only three bedrooms – and since it's close to the river, there's no basement."

"That makes sense," Eric said. "It's good you brought me along in case things get dangerous."

Harper bit her tongue to keep from laughing. Eric was a good guy – a whiz with the computer equipment – but he'd never been in the thick of things when a ghost got out of hand. "I agree. So, back to Molly ... ."

"Oh, right," Eric said. "I don't know what to think about her right now. Ever since it happened she's been ... unpredictable."

"You see her more than I do," Harper reminded him. "Be specific."

"You're not going to fire her, are you?" Eric asked, his face earnest.

"She's young and she says stupid things, but … I don't want you to fire her."

Harper was floored. "Do you really think I would fire her because she's going through a rough time after being drugged, kidnapped, and almost killed?"

"No," Eric replied hurriedly. "It's just … she's sad, and I'm worried you think that's going to get in the way of her doing her job. It won't. She needs a little more time and then she'll get over it."

Harper stilled. "What do you mean she's sad?"

"Haven't you looked at her recently?"

"I look at her every chance I get," Harper replied. "I'm worried sick about her. I don't want to push her, so I sit there and stare at her and try to think of ways to help her."

"That's the exact wrong thing to do," Eric said. "You need to treat her like you used to treat her. Make fun of her … tease her … tell her to shut up a time or two. That's what she needs."

Harper knit her eyebrows together. "Are you just saying that because you like being mean to her?"

"I don't like being mean to her," Eric protested. "She likes to argue, though. I like to argue, too. I'm giving her what she wants when I'm mean to her. No one has been arguing with her since she was hurt."

"She was more than hurt. She was almost killed."

"So were you and Zander, and you two were arguing the next day," Eric pointed out. "You keep treating Molly as if she's breakable. If you continue doing that, sooner or later she's going to decide she's broken."

The statement was almost profound in its simplicity.

"I didn't really think about that," Harper admitted. "I thought she was dead. Collin told me she was dead. When Mel said they found her alive … I was so relieved."

"I think that you and Zander know how to treat one another because you're the same age and you've been friends forever," Eric said. "Molly is younger, but all she really wants is to be treated like one of the group. Is there a reason you can't treat her like one of the group?"

"I thought we were. You take care of the people in your group. We've been trying to take care of her."

"No. You've been trying to coddle her," Eric corrected. "You've been treating her as if she's special and needs a mother, not a friend. You're not her mother. She has a mother to coddle her. You need to be her friend and treat her like an equal. That's all she really wants."

Harper rubbed the back of her neck as she considered Eric's words. "That's a pretty keen observation."

"I do my best," Eric replied dryly.

"I think you're smarter than we give you credit for sometimes," Harper said.

"In that case ... I don't think you should date Jared because he's going to hurt you again," Eric said, causing Harper to swallow a groan.

"Let's see if we can find a ghost, shall we?" Harper asked, veering away from Eric's pointed statement as fast as humanly possible. "You check that side of the house and I'll check this one."

"I can't see ghosts."

"I ... well ... see if you can start," Harper suggested.

"HOW DID things go with Harper last night?" Mel asked, pulling into the parking lot of the local high school and killing his cruiser's engine. "Did you two make up?"

"Kind of," Jared replied, pushing open his door and climbing out.

Mel joined him on the pavement and fixed him with a dark look over the cruiser when they were both outside. "Kind of?"

"She's being a pain," Jared admitted. "She wants to make up and yet she's digging her heels in. I can't decide if it's a woman thing or a Harper thing. She's still kind of a mystery to me."

Mel chuckled softly. "That's a woman thing, son. Trust me. Harper isn't some weird and wonderful creature where stuff like that is concerned. She's not an anomaly. Did she give you any leeway?"

"Well, she told me to have a nice day outside of GHI, so I grabbed her and kissed the crap out her," Jared said. "That went on for like ten minutes while Zander and the other two watched from inside and ate all the candy I bought her."

Mel snorted. "That sounds about right. Then what happened?"

"Then I took her to the park so we could look for Derek's ghost."

"And?"

"And we had a big fight about why I didn't call," Jared replied. "I explained in excruciating detail what happened and she felt a little better. Then I held her hand and watched her work. She's still not thrilled with me, but I told her she was going to have to forgive me today no matter what. I guess that means I'm going to have to make dinner for her and Zander – although I'd much rather have a private dinner than a threesome once she thinks I'm cute again."

Jared glanced at Mel and found his partner glowering in his direction. "What?"

"I wasn't asking for the down-and-dirty details of your pseudo date with Harper just now," Mel said. "I was asking what you found when you went to the park in regards to Derek and his death."

"Oh," Jared said, realization dawning and causing his cheeks to burn. "Well, in that case, forget I told you all that mushy stuff about my night with Harper."

"I wish I could forget it."

"Derek showed up and was ... surly," Jared said.

"What does that mean?" Mel asked, confused. "Derek was always pleasant when I talked to him."

"That's because he was a teenage suck-up and you were a cop who was friends with his parents," Jared said. "He knew you would tattle on him the first chance you got if it became necessary, so he snowed you whenever he was in the same room."

"You don't know that," Mel charged. "He could've looked up to me. A lot of people do."

"I'm sure they do," Jared replied dryly. "He called Harper a 'dippy blonde' and mentioned something about her hanging around with your gay nephew. She tried to ask him what happened, but he said he couldn't remember."

"And you're convinced she was talking to Derek and not air, right?" Mel asked, giving Jared a glimpse of his own surliness.

"You believed she could see ghosts yesterday," Jared reminded him. "Is there a reason you're turning on her today?"

"Derek was a good kid," Mel replied, lowering his voice. "I don't like her calling him 'surly.'"

"She didn't refer to him that way," Jared volunteered. "I did."

"You couldn't see or hear him."

"I could hear Harper talking to him, and she told me what he said during the drive home," Jared explained. "I got the gist of what she was saying without her having to tell me, though."

"Maybe Harper is crazy. Have you ever thought about that?"

"Don't call my girlfriend crazy," Jared warned.

Mel made a face that would've been comical under different circumstances. "She's barely talking to you and now you're referring to her as your girlfriend? How does that work?"

"She's going to forgive me."

"You hope."

"I know," Jared corrected. "Don't talk badly about her. I don't like it."

Mel's somber expression slipped into a smile. "Fine. You're right. I shouldn't talk badly about her. She's a good girl … even if she is crazy."

"If you say it again I'm going to tell Zander you were talking badly about his best friend," Jared threatened. "Not only will that earn me points with him, but it will also get you in big trouble with your sister when Zander tells her what you've been doing."

Jared was new to the Whisper Cove game and yet he already knew exactly where to hit Mel and make it hurt.

"That's low," Mel said. "You're my partner. You're supposed to be on my side."

"Then don't say anything bad about my girl."

"You're unbelievable," Mel said, shaking his head and moving toward the school. "You haven't even been out on an official date with Harper yet. Don't you think you're moving too fast?"

"It feels as if I'm stuck in quicksand," Jared admitted, falling into step with Mel. "I need her to forgive me today. I think I'm going to have to cook her dinner. Zander is demanding steak and wine that doesn't come from a box."

Mel heartily guffawed. "Yeah. One of our cousins brought wine in a box to a reunion two years ago. He's still bellyaching about it. He has high standards."

"Of course he does. He's best friends with Harper."

"Son, you're starting to sound sappy and whipped," Mel said, gesturing toward the front door of the school and holding it open so Jared could slip inside ahead of him. "I haven't seen a lovesick pup like yourself since I was in high school."

"Get used to it," Jared said. "Once I get Harper to forgive me, I'm going to be talking about her nonstop."

"And that differs from now how?"

Jared shrugged. "Hopefully they'll be happier conversations."

"That would be a nice change of pace."

NINE

Whisper Cove's guidance counselor Jim Stone waited in the front lobby for Mel and Jared to appear. They'd called ahead of time so he was expecting them.

"Hey, Mel," Jim said, shaking the older officer's hand. "It's good to see you. I wish it was under different circumstances."

"You and me both," Mel said. "This is my new partner Jared Monroe. Jared, this is Jim Stone. If anything is going on in Whisper Cove's high school scene, Jim here knows about it."

Jared shook the guidance counselor's proffered hand. "It's nice to meet you."

"You, too," Jim said. "I've heard a lot about you since you hit town. You're cream of the gossip crop right now. You should be proud."

Jared wasn't sure what to make of that. "Really?"

Jim smiled. "There's a rumor you're dating Harper Harlow. Is that true?"

Mel snickered. "Oh, man. I forgot you had a crush on Harper, Jim. That's going back ten years now since you guys were in high school together. Don't you think it's about time to let that go?"

"I never did get that date I always wanted with her," Jim replied, his eyes twinkling. "I'm still holding out hope she'll realize I'm the man of her dreams and drop everything and run into my arms."

Jared fought his bristling temper. He had no reason to dislike Jim. He was merely making a joke about a woman he went to high school with. The knowledge that Jim had a thing for Harper set Jared's teeth on edge for some reason, although he tried to play it off. "We're dating," he said. "I guess you missed out again."

Mel arched a challenging eyebrow. "Since when are you two officially dating?"

"We will be dating once she gets over being ticked off," Jared clarified. "We're ... pre-dating."

Jim chortled. "I didn't know that was a thing outside of teenage circles," he said, gesturing toward the hallway. "Let's take this to my office, shall we? There aren't a lot of kids hanging around, but we do have a few derelicts who have to attend classes or they won't graduate."

"I thought school was done for the summer break," Jared said, scanning the hallway as they moved through the school. Whisper Cove was tiny, which meant the high school was practically miniscule. Still, Jared found it interesting to catch a glimpse of the inner workings of the school when it felt mostly empty.

"Well, yes and no," Jim said, showing Jared and Mel into his office and shutting the door to lock out prying ears. "We technically finished classes last Friday. Instead of hosting summer school, though, the faculty stays on two extra weeks so we can prod the last few lazy students to catch up. It's just easier on everyone to stay rather than come back."

"That makes sense."

"So, are you really dating Harper?" Jim asked.

"I really am," Jared replied, scowling when Mel cleared his throat. "Stop doing that."

"He wants to be dating Harper," Mel clarified. "He had a good shot at it before he ticked her off. Now she's playing hard to get ... although he's determined to get her."

"And what do you think?" Jim asked.

Mel shrugged, noncommittal. "If I had to place a bet ... I would put my money on him. He and Harper seem to like each other ... when she's not mad."

Jim shook his head ruefully. "That's kind of a bummer. I was hoping to have a shot with Harper one day."

"You went to high school with Harper?" Jared asked, hoping he didn't sound as territorial as he felt. He had no idea why Jim's teasing interest in Harper caused his hackles to go up.

"I did," Jim said. "She was quiet and kept to herself mostly, although Zander was gregarious and refused to let her completely disappear. They were joined at the hip even then. It drove me nuts."

"They're still joined at the hip," Mel said. "Zander can't pick out his clothes in the morning without Harper's input, and they fight like cats and dogs whenever the mood strikes."

"I still maintain I would've had a shot with Harper if Zander didn't hate me," Jim lamented.

"Why did Zander hate you?" Jared asked, curiosity getting the better of him.

"I mixed plaids and stripes one spring."

"Oh," Jared said, furrowing his brow. "I ... seriously?"

"No," Jim said, slapping his knee as he laughed. "It's funny that you fell for that, though. I've told that joke so many times most people roll their eyes."

"Jared is still getting used to Harper and Zander's dynamic," Mel explained. "He doesn't completely get their unique blend of codependence yet."

"Zander and I had a ... misunderstanding ... senior year," Jim explained. "I was on the football team and some of the other guys were razzing him about ... ." Jim broke off, unsure. "It really sounds horrible now."

Jared had a feeling he knew what the football team was "razzing" Zander about, and he didn't like it. "I'm taking it Harper didn't take that well."

"That's one of the few times I saw her completely lose control," Jim said. "I didn't go after Zander, but I didn't do anything to stop the other guys from going after him. I was a coward and … well … Harper doesn't like cowards. I asked her to the spring dance two days later and she threatened to set me on fire. I've never gotten over it."

Despite himself, Jared couldn't help but smile. "Well, I'm sure you regret it now."

"I do," Jim agreed, nodding. "I regret it more because of Zander than Harper, though. When you're young and looking at things from a narrow perspective you don't realize the damage you're doing until it's too late to fix it."

"Whisper Cove is – and was – a small town," he continued. "Zander was different, and I thought that meant something at the time. Now that I'm an adult and sitting on the other side of this desk I can see how wrong I was."

"You could apologize to Zander," Jared suggested. "He'd probably appreciate it now. He's an adult. He must understand that you were a kid and you didn't mean for anything to happen."

"Oh, I've tried apologizing to Zander three times," Jim said. "Each time Harper gets between us and threatens to set me on fire again."

Jared visibly relaxed. "She's feisty."

"She is," Jim agreed. "Good luck with her. I hope she forgives you. She hasn't threatened to set you on fire, has she?"

Jared shook his head. "I guess I'm not that lucky."

"Not that I don't love talking about Harper and her feisty personality – for days on end, mind you – but we're here to talk about Derek Thompson," Mel prodded. "I need to know what you can tell me about him."

"Yeah, that's a terrible thing," Jim said, leafing through the file on his desk. "I pulled his file after I got your call. There's not a lot in here because he wasn't a troublemaker. He had a few detentions for being rowdy, but nothing even remotely serious."

"He was a good kid," Mel said, starting to sound like a broken record.

"I don't know what you want me to tell you," Jim admitted. "Derek was popular with the boys and girls. He was active on the football and track teams, and he tore through a lot of the female population before settling on Lexie Studebaker. He was with her for half the year ... and I think they were still together when he died, although I'm not a hundred percent positive."

"What kind of relationship did they have?" Jared asked.

Jim shrugged. "That's always hard to say because teenagers are the kings and queens of drama," he answered. "The problem you have with kids this age is that they feel things so keenly they're convinced it's love and that it's going to last forever.

"When I was in high school most of the girls thought they were going to marry their prom dates," he continued. "Do you know how many did? Two. Do you know how many of those are still married? None. It's ... very theatrical. That's the one thing that never changes about high school."

"What aren't you trying to say?" Jared prodded. "Now isn't the time to be coy. Derek is dead and there's a good chance he was murdered."

Jim stilled. "You don't know how he died?"

"We know he died from a blow to the head," Mel replied. "The problem is we're still trying to ascertain if he fell or was hit. The medical examiner is going over the toxicology results right now and we should know more in a few hours ... tomorrow at the latest."

"I don't know how to feel about that," Jim admitted. "These kids believe they're immortal, so an accident will elicit a different sort of drama than a murder."

"Go back to Lexie," Jared ordered. "Tell us about their relationship. It's okay. We're not going to go after her because of something you say. We're trying to get a feel for his life away from his parents."

"Lexie is a cheerleader who thinks she's going to be on top of the world for the rest of her life," Jim explained. "She's very pretty ... and she knows it. She doesn't particularly seem ... dialed in, I guess would be the proper way to put it ... to what others are feeling."

"What does that mean?" Mel asked, confused.

"I think he's saying she's a bully," Jared supplied.

Jim shot Jared a rueful smile. "That's putting it nicely," he said. "Lexie finds power in tearing others down. She's been validated for two straight years as queen of the Whisper Cove social scene. I think she's going to get a rude awakening when she goes off to college and realizes she's a no one in a sea of other no ones, but until then she enjoys torturing others."

"Can you be more specific?"

"Well, she makes fun of kids for the way they dress and if their parents can't afford the right shoes," Jim responded. "Whisper Cove isn't a rich community. It's not a poor one, though, either. Lexie seems to unilaterally decide what is cool and everyone just … lets her."

"How did she and Derek hook up?"

"I have no idea. I'm into the gossip scene, but even I'm not into it that far. I just know they hooked up over Christmas break and decided to rule the school together for the second half of the year."

Mel narrowed his eyes. "What does that mean?"

"Derek was a good kid," Jim said. "He also had a mean streak and he was very competitive. He and Lexie fed off each other. I was glad they were accepted to different colleges because I think some separation would've been good for them."

"Derek was going to Central Michigan University," Mel explained for Jared's benefit. "Where is Lexie going?"

"She got accepted to Western Michigan University … but just barely," Jim replied. "In fact, she's had some academic problems. She's one of the students here this week to make up for a few … lapses … during the school year."

"What kind of lapses?" Jared asked.

"Lexie is a smart girl who doesn't want to apply herself," Jim said. "She thought she could coast through on looks and what she thinks is charm, and then she was waitlisted at Western. Apparently her father placed a call … and gave a hefty donation … and she suddenly found herself part of the student body. She still hasn't received her diploma because she failed algebra, though, so her attendance at Western is contingent on passing the next two weeks here."

"And that's what she's doing right now?" Jared pressed. "Algebra?"

"She and a few other students failed algebra because they rubbed Dan Stevens the wrong way," Jim offered. "He retired at the end of the year and his replacement is running the auxiliary classes this week and next."

"How many kids in that class were tight with Derek?"

"I think most of them were," Jim said, searching his memory. "I can take you down there if you want. It will probably be easier to question them in a contained environment."

"That would be helpful," Jared said. "Is there anything else you can tell us about Derek before we talk to the kids?"

"Just that I think he would've outgrown his small-town mentality and realized what was important eventually," Jim said. "At his heart, Derek was a good kid who sometimes made bad decisions. Since I know what it's like to make bad decisions when you're that age and live to regret them, I saw a lot of potential in him."

"But not in Lexie?"

"I don't want to say she's a bad person," Jim cautioned. "She's just … got a lot of growing up to do. You can tell when someone is a fully formed human as a teenager. Lexie is nowhere near being a fully formed human yet. She's … eons … away."

"Well, I can't wait to meet her," Jared said.

"You probably won't be saying that in twenty minutes. Come on. I think they're all eating lunch in the courtyard right now."

TEN

"So … why are we at the high school?" Eric asked, nervously hurrying to catch Harper as she cut across the field between the high school and downtown. "I thought we were supposed to check out that house and then go back to the office."

"Yes, but it's boring at the office and I want to see if anyone who might know Derek Thompson is up at the high school," Harper replied, undaunted by Eric's quiet meltdown. He was convinced they were trespassing, and no matter how many times Harper told him the high school was public property, he refused to believe her.

After their fruitless search at Tina Donnelly's old place – the elderly woman passed away almost six months before and her heirs were trying to unload it for the inheritance – Harper bought Eric lunch and spent the next hour trying to direct him toward any topic of conversation that didn't involve Jared. Since she couldn't find a ghost at the cottage, that endeavor proved harder than she would've liked.

She knew what Eric wanted, and it wasn't something she couldn't give him. While she liked Eric as a friend – and found him wonderfully entertaining at times – she wasn't interested in him in a romantic sense. Unfortunately, there was only one man she felt that way about ... and she was determined to remain angry with him no matter how cute he was.

"Why are we involved in the Derek Thompson case?" Eric asked, furtively glancing around. "We could get arrested because we're old and on a high school campus. You know that, right?"

"Mel and Jared are the two top cops in town," Harper replied. "Do you think either one of them is going to arrest me?"

"I think Jared would threaten to arrest you if you refuse to go out with him," Eric suggested, causing Harper to scowl.

"You need to let the Jared thing go," Harper instructed. "You're starting to make me uncomfortable because you're so obsessed with him. Maybe you should go out with him since he's all you can think about."

"He's not all I think about," Eric muttered.

Harper pretended she didn't hear him. "If you don't want to question the kids with me, you're more than welcome to go back to the office. I can walk back by myself. It's less than a mile."

Eric balked. "We came together. We should leave together."

"I guess it's settled then," Harper said, rounding the corner that led to the front of the building and pulling up short when she saw a handful of teenagers sitting at a picnic table next to the building. "Huh."

"Huh what?" Eric asked.

"I expected to find kids at the basketball court in the parking lot," Harper explained. "School is out. Why are they here?"

"Maybe they're in summer school."

Harper brightened. "That means they're probably dumb and will answer any questions I have. Come on. Teenage boys love me."

Harper approached the kids with a wide smile and her best "you can trust me" expression. "Hi, guys."

The three boys and one girl looked up, instantly mistrustful. *So much for my teenage appeal*, Harper internally lamented.

"You're not supposed to be here," the girl said. Harper recognized her as Lexie Studebaker. "If you're trolling for men, all the ones here are illegal."

One of the boys, Dylan Walsh, raised his hand. "I'm eighteen and you can troll for me. I'll take one for the team."

Harper frowned. "Listen … ."

"I'm eighteen, too," Brandon Sanders said. "You're hot. If you're looking for someone to teach a few lessons to, I'm your guy. I love to learn."

"That must be why you're here for summer school," David Martin said, the sun glinting off his watch. "You just love to learn." He winked at Harper for good measure. "I'm not eighteen yet – although I'm only two weeks away from being legal. I promise not to tell anyone if you want to teach me a few things."

"Don't be rude," Eric ordered, causing the boys to snicker.

"You guys are funny," Harper said. "I forgot how funny high school boys were."

"That's because you're old," Lexie said. "I mean … where do you shop? It looks like Old Navy."

Harper glanced down at her simple jeans and T-shirt. That was a pretty good guess. She was more interested in comfort than fashion. For someone like Lexie, who was wearing Jimmy Choo sandals, Old Navy was probably a step down – or possibly ten steps down – the fashion ladder. "I'm here to ask you guys a few questions about Derek Thompson," she said, opting not to beat around the bush. The less time she had to spend with these kids, the better. "Were any of you close with him?"

Lexie took the opportunity to wrinkle her nose and burst into tears, earning a hug from Brandon as she leaned into him.

"Should I take that as a yes?"

"Lexie and Derek were dating," Dylan explained. "She's crushed."

"We were in love," Lexie wailed.

Harper's heart went out to the girl … and then immediately retracted. There was something fake about Lexie's anguish, although Harper couldn't quite put her finger on why she felt that way. "I'm truly sorry."

"No, you're not," Lexie shot back. "You don't look sorry."

"I'll draw a sad face on later," Harper said, turning her attention to

Dylan. He seemed the most receptive to her presence. "Do any of you guys know what he was doing out at the park the night before last?"

Dylan shrugged. "I have no idea," he answered. "We spent some time out there when it was warm ... you know, just chilling and not doing anything illegal ... but I have no idea why he was out there that night. We weren't supposed to meet or anything."

Harper internally rolled her eyes at the "not doing anything illegal" part. These guys had "underage drinking" written all over them. She didn't really care how they partied, but she didn't want to encourage them either. "Do you guys know anyone who was hanging around the park that night?"

Dylan shook his head.

"Did Derek have any enemies?"

"Why are you asking these questions?" Lexie asked, her shoulders shaking as she lifted her damp eyes to Harper and scorched her with a harsh look. "Why are you even here?"

"That's a pretty good question."

Harper froze when she heard the new voice, briefly pressing her eyes shut and swiveling to find Jared, Mel, and Jim Stone staring at her.

"Hello, Harper," Mel said, his voice full of faux brightness. "What are you doing here?"

"Hi, Harper," Jim offered, shuffling worriedly.

"I'll still set you on fire," Harper hissed, narrowing her eyes.

Jared smirked and leaned closer to Jim. "I'll pay you a hundred bucks if you let me punch you. She's bound to forgive me once I do that."

Jim rolled his eyes while Harper glared at Jared.

"What are you guys doing here?" Harper asked, turning the question around on them while she thought of a passable answer to appease Mel.

"We're doing our job," Mel replied, unruffled. "We're here to talk to the kids about Derek. Back to you."

"Um ... ."

"I didn't want to come," Eric announced, holding his hands up as if

74

to prove he wasn't in possession of a weapon. "I told her it was a bad idea."

Jared ran his tongue over his teeth as he tried not to laugh. Eric looked as if he wanted a hole to open up and swallow him alive and Harper was getting more defiant by the second.

"I think she's here to pick up boys," Lexie said. "I told her she was too old, but these guys keep flirting with her and she thinks she has a shot. Personally, I think it's just cruel to play with people's emotions like that."

"Oh, shut up," Harper said. "You know very well I'm not here to pick up teenage boys."

"I volunteered to take one for the team," Dylan said. "I can vouch for her. She didn't take me up on my offer."

"She didn't turn us down either," Brandon pointed out.

Mel chuckled hoarsely. "Are you expanding your dating pool now that you've washed your hands of my partner, Harper? Is that what you're doing here?"

"Don't push me," Jared muttered, edging around Mel and moving closer to Harper. He knew exactly what she was doing at the school. "Did you get anywhere with your questions?"

Harper tilted her head to the side, her blond hair dipping low as she considered how to respond. He wasn't acting angry. That was a bonus. Of course, he could be pretending so she would forgive him. It was probably a trap. "I only asked a few before that one started crying and making a scene," she replied, gesturing toward Lexie.

"I'm in mourning," Lexie said. "She's the one trying to pick up teenage boys and molest them."

"Stop saying that," Harper seethed. "What is your deal?"

"She's a teenage girl," Jim supplied helpfully. "She likes pressing people's buttons. You remember what it was like to be that age, right? You say and do things you don't mean. Most of the time you grow out of those things and move past them … well, if people ever let you move past them."

Jared watched Harper for her reaction. He wasn't disappointed.

"Some things shouldn't be let go," Harper said.

"I think you've tortured him long enough," Mel interjected. "Zander is my nephew. He let this grudge go a long time ago. It's been ten years, Harper. Don't you think it's time to let bygones be bygones?"

"Yeah," Lexie said, her voice unnaturally high. "Forgive him. He's your age and you won't get arrested if you date him."

"She's not dating him," Jared interjected.

"You don't know that," Harper argued. "I could date him if I wanted to."

Jim looked intrigued and puffed his chest out. "I would love to take you to dinner."

"Now I'm going to punch you and not give you a hundred bucks," Jared warned.

"Yeah, I'm not going out to dinner with you," Harper added. "I just don't want Jared thinking it's because of him." She risked a glance at Eric and found him smiling, something akin to victory washing over his handsome features. She had a feeling she just made things worse. "On the other hand, well, maybe I will go out with Jared. I'm hungry and he owes me a good dinner."

"You can't go out with him," Lexie said, making a face. "He's too hot for you."

"Hey!"

"Oh, she's going out with me," Jared said. "I'm going to give her the best dinner money can buy, and then she's going to realize she has absolutely no reason to be angry with me."

"Wait, what happened to you going out with me?" Jim asked. "I liked that idea better."

"I will arrest you," Jared threatened, his voice low.

"On what charge?"

"Moving in on my turf," Jared replied, not missing a beat.

"As wonderfully immature as this all is, can we get back to the topic at hand?" Mel asked, refusing to let hormones dictate the conversation for one more second. "We have an important investigation. Your ... dating life ... is something that should be handled when you're off the clock."

"I technically set my own clock, so that doesn't apply to me," Harper sniffed.

"I'm off at five," Jim interjected.

"No one asked you," Jared said.

Mel scowled and turned back to the kids. "Can anyone give me a reason why Derek Thompson was out at the town park the night before last?"

Everyone shook their heads in unison, causing Mel to focus on Lexie.

"I understand you and Derek were dating," he said, his voice filling with sympathy and warmth. "When was the last time you talked to him?"

Now that she was the center of attention, Lexie's bad attitude shifted faster than her earlier tears dried. "We talked that night around ten," she answered. "We were making plans for the next day. He didn't say anything about going out."

"Was it uncommon for him to go out that late?" Jared asked, returning to the matter at hand, but keeping an eye on Harper to make sure she didn't bolt before he had a chance to firm up their dinner plans. "Did he usually go out after dark alone?"

"I don't think so," Lexie answered. "If he did, he never told me."

"Did he confide in you a lot?"

"He told me everything," Lexie said, her cheeks glowing with the naïve flush of youth. "We were going to be together forever."

Harper zeroed in on Brandon, who rolled his eyes during Lexie's declaration. Apparently he didn't believe her statement any more than Harper did.

"Can anyone think of a person who would want to hurt Derek?" Mel asked, his tone grave. "This is important. Even if you think it was a minor misunderstanding, we need to know if Derek had any enemies."

"Derek was loved by everyone," Lexie said solemnly. "He was loved by me most of all, though. He didn't have any enemies."

Mel glanced at the boys. "Do you agree with that?"

"Derek was the most popular kid in school," Dylan replied. "There's absolutely no reason anyone would want to hurt him."

For some reason, everything about that statement felt false to Harper. She wisely kept that observation to herself, though.

After a few more questions, Mel dismissed the kids and told them to return to the building. Jim made one more half-hearted attempt to apologize to Harper – and ask her out – but he was met with icy stares, so he finally gave up and led Mel inside to go over Derek's file.

Eric tugged on Harper's arm to get her to leave, frantically trying to pull her away before Jared could approach. The cop stopped him before he had a chance to achieve his goal.

"If you have somewhere to be, Eric, I'll walk Harper back to the office," Jared offered.

"No ... I ... no." Eric shook his head.

"In that case, can you give Harper and me a moment to talk?" Jared asked, his eyes flashing with warning in case Eric tried to put up a fight.

"Sure," Eric replied, dejectedly kicking at the ground as he moved several feet away.

"Well, that got us absolutely nowhere," Harper grumbled when it was just the two of them.

"I don't know. I feel like I got somewhere."

Harper wanted to scowl, but Jared's grin was so cute she couldn't help but return it. "You're starting to wear me down. We both know it."

"I *do* know it," Jared agreed. "That's why I want you to go to dinner with me tonight."

"I thought you were supposed to cook Zander dinner first?" Harper challenged.

"I want our first official date to be just the two of us," Jared replied. "I will cook Zander the dinner of his dreams once we've had a chance to spend time together and I know you're okay being with me again."

Harper sighed. "I really want to be mad at you."

"That's what your head says," Jared countered. "What does your heart say?"

"I'll meet you at the steakhouse on Gratiot at seven." Harper gave in. It was only a matter of time. She didn't want to fight his pull for one moment longer than necessary. It was too much effort.

"I'll pick you up at your house at seven," Jared corrected. "We're going on a proper date. That means I'm walking to your front door to collect you and opening the car door for you. That's what you do on a proper date."

Warmth spread through Harper's stomach. "Does that mean I have to wear a skirt?"

Jared grinned. "Those are the rules."

"I'll see you at seven."

ELEVEN

"How do I look?" Harper's hands shook as she stood in front of Zander thirty minutes before Jared was due to arrive. "Do I look desperate?"

Zander glanced up from the magazine he was perusing on the couch. "You look like a school teacher."

"Is that good?"

"Let me rephrase that," Zander said. "You look like a school teacher from *Little House on the Prairie*. What was her name? We used to love that show."

"Are you saying I look like Miss Beadle?"

"Miss Beadle!" Zander slapped his knee. "I loved her. I loved that episode where Mary thought she was never going to attract a man because all the other kids made fun of her glasses and then Miss Beadle showed up with a boyfriend we never saw again and Mary realized men like women who wear glasses."

"Wow. That's thirty seconds of my life I'll never get back," Harper deadpanned. "Did you have a point with that little diatribe?"

Zander's expression softened. "You're nervous and it shows. You're so cute."

"You're not helping me!" Harper exploded.

Zander made an exaggerated face and tossed the magazine on the couch. "You need to take it down a notch," he said, getting to his feet. "I'm here to help you. This is why I told you to get dressed early. I knew you would pick the wrong outfit and need my expertise."

"I've been dressing myself since I was eight."

"And I've been redressing you since we were twelve," Zander countered. "Come on." He stalked into Harper's bedroom, glancing at the mountain of clothes on the middle of her bed before turning toward the closet. "We should've gone shopping when Jared was out of town and gotten you something sexier to wear. Your clothing options are tragic."

Harper watched as he pulled a few items out and made faces. "Zander ... ."

Something about the way she said his name caused Zander to look up. He knew Harper as well as he knew himself, and he was keenly aware of the anxiety rolling through her. "Harp, it's going to be okay," he said, his expression softening. "Jared likes you. You like Jared. This is a good thing."

"But ... ."

Zander shook his head. "No. You want this. I know you do. You need to get over yourself and let it happen."

"What if he changes his mind?"

"You just spent two days torturing the man and he kept coming back for more abuse," Zander pointed out. "He's not going to change his mind. I ... suck in a breath, Harp. Sit down."

Harper did as instructed, fanning herself as her face reddened. "I think I really like him."

"I know you really like him," Zander said. "Harp, tell me what's really going on? Are you nervous because of Jared, or are you afraid because you haven't had sex in so long you're worried everything has changed?"

Harper's mouth dropped open. "We are not having sex tonight!"

"I wish you would," Zander countered. "If we have to go through this every single time you two go out on a date, you're going to give me an aneurysm. I want to get everything out and in the open as fast as possible. You shaved your legs just in case, right?"

"Yes," Harper admitted, mortified. "I even used that Body Shop margarita lotion you got me."

"Good girl," Zander said, pulling her in for a quick hug. "I promise this is going to be okay." His voice was barely a whisper as he rubbed her back. "This is going to be good for you."

Harper sucked in a steadying breath. "What should I wear?"

"You don't have a lot of options," Zander replied. "You're going to have to wear this black skirt and this purple top." He pressed the clothing items into her hands. "Put those on and then I'll fix your hair."

"What's wrong with my hair?"

"Nothing once I fix your makeup, too," Zander said. "Now ... come on. You've got a man coming and you're running out of time. Chop, chop."

JARED WIPED his sweaty palms on the front of his trousers before lifting his hand to knock on Harper's door. He was taken aback when the door opened and he found Zander staring out at him. For some reason it made him feel better knowing Zander was about to give him grief. That would take the edge off.

"I'll make your dinner another night," Jared said. "Tonight I want it to be just her and me."

"I don't care about that," Zander said, pushing Jared out onto the porch and silently shutting the door. "She's still getting ready. It's been ... freaking drama."

"What's wrong?" Jared's stomach twisted with worry. Was Harper going to cancel the date? "If she's trying to back out ... let me talk to her."

"She's not going to back out," Zander said, keeping his voice low. "She's so excited she can barely contain herself."

"So what's wrong?"

"She's going to be nervous for the first half hour," Zander

cautioned. "Talk to her like you normally would and try to pretend you don't notice her acting odd."

The realization that Harper was more worked up than he was relieved some of the tension building in Jared's heart. "How does she look?"

"I have to take her shopping."

"That's not what I asked."

"She looks beautiful," Zander said. "She always does. She doesn't see that about herself sometimes. You'd better tell her."

Jared scowled. "Thank you for the dating tips."

"Make sure she eats something," Zander instructed. "She's going to do that girl thing and order something cheap … or a salad … but she needs fuel so make sure she eats something hearty."

Jared nodded. "Anything else, Dad?"

"Yes," Zander replied, not missing a beat. "I'm going out on my own date. If something goes wrong, she's going to balk at calling me. Make sure she calls me if she starts panicking."

"Why would she panic?" Jared asked. "It's a date. I'm not going to pressure her into doing something she doesn't want to do."

"That's very nice," Zander deadpanned. "She shaved her legs and she's good to go on that front. You bring her back here to do that because she'll be more comfortable in her own home. I probably won't be back until tomorrow morning if she doesn't call, so you'll have the house to yourself."

Jared was dumbfounded. Was Zander really telling him to make a move on the first date? "Don't you think it's a little soon for that?"

"No."

"Okay, I'll bite," Jared said. "Why would I push her to do that tonight?"

"Because it's the one thing that's going to relax her," Zander answered. "We're going to go through this ten more times if you don't wow her now. So … get her naked and do your thing." Zander patted Jared's back. "You'd better be good in bed, too. If you're bad after all this build up I'll never hear the end of it."

"Well, that's not putting too much pressure on me or anything," Jared grumbled.

"She looks like a dream and you clean up well, too," Zander said. "She's the love of my life and I will beat the crap out of you if you hurt her."

"Duly noted."

"You still owe me a home-cooked dinner, too," Zander added. "Now ... go and make my girl happy. I'm counting on you."

Jared's heart rolled at the emotion flitting through Zander's eyes. The love reflected there was nothing short of amazing. "That's all I want."

"I know. That's why I like you."

"**THIS** IS A NICE RESTAURANT," Jared said, pulling Harper's chair out and making sure she was settled before sitting across from her. "Have you eaten here before?"

Despite her earlier nerves, once she was in Jared's truck Harper managed to relax. Jared matched her nervous glance for nervous glance during the drive, and she couldn't help but be relieved. "Zander and I ate here once a few years ago," she said. "He declared the steak 'to die for.'"

"That sounds good," Jared said. "You can't come to a steakhouse and not have steak."

Harper was conflicted. "I was thinking of maybe getting a salad," she said, flipping open the menu.

"No, you weren't," Jared shot back. "You're having a big dinner and I don't want to hear one argument about it."

Harper pursed her lips. "What did you and Zander talk about on the front porch tonight?"

Jared feigned ignorance. "What do you mean?"

"You were out there for five minutes before you came inside," Harper said. "Don't bother lying. I saw Zander sneak out and head you off before you could knock. What did he say to you?"

"He said if I hurt you he was going to kill me."

"That's it?" Harper was surprised. "He didn't say anything about me?"

"He said that he wished he'd taken you shopping – although I think you look beautiful and he's being dramatic – and that I still owed him dinner," Jared replied. None of those things were lies. If she pressed him on the rest of his conversation with Zander things would be uncomfortable.

"You look handsome," Harper said, looking him up and down appreciatively. "I've never seen you out of your jeans and button-down shirts."

"I don't dress up a lot," Jared said. "I like to be comfortable. This is a special occasion, though."

"I'm surprised you still wanted to go out with me after I was mean to you."

"I'm surprised you said yes after I was such an idiot."

Harper bit her lip to keep from laughing, and then gave in. "I was nervous earlier. You have a way of putting me at ease, though. I can't explain it."

"I was nervous, too," Jared admitted. "I'm still a little nervous, but I wouldn't want to be anywhere but here with you."

The waitress picked that moment to arrive, and after placing their orders Jared turned to the next order of business. "I want to know everything about you."

Harper snorted. "That's ... not going to take up very much of the night."

"Well, I'll direct you where I want to start then," Jared said. "Tell me what the deal is with Eric."

Harper balked. "What do you mean? He's my employee. He's a good guy."

"I'm not saying he's not a good guy," Jared said. "It's obvious he has a crush on you, though. It's not the first time I've noticed it. He almost had a meltdown when we talked about going on a date earlier."

"He's just ... trying to find himself," Harper explained. "He looks at me and thinks I'm exotic because of the ghost thing. He's a few years younger than me and ignores clues ... like the fact that I'm not sexually attracted to him. If he would turn around for five seconds he would see that Molly *is* attracted to him and she adores everything he does."

"How is Molly?"

"I think I've been too overprotective," Harper replied. "Eric and I had to go out and survey a house that's up for sale because the real estate agent is convinced it's haunted and we talked about Molly today. He says I've been coddling her when she really just wants to be part of the group. I think he's right."

"Was the house haunted?" Jared was intrigued by Harper's ghost vision. He couldn't deny it.

"Not that I saw," Harper answered. "I think the real estate agent – her name is Jenny Porter, we went to high school together – is looking for an excuse why she hasn't sold the cottage yet. She claims things keep moving around, but I didn't see anything."

"What keeps moving around?"

"Mostly dishes. I think she's just looking for an excuse."

"Well, I like how honest you are," Jared said. "Someone else in your position might claim a ghost is there and take money to do nothing. I'd like to go with you on a job one day … if you're okay with that."

Harper was surprised. "You would? Really?"

"I want to see all of it, Harper. I want to … do … all of it with you."

Harper's cheeks colored. "Sometimes I think you're too good to be true."

"Even though I was a moron and didn't call you?"

"Even though," Harper said.

The duo eyed each other for a moment, something sweet passing between them before the heat ratcheted up a notch. Suddenly Jared wasn't so sure Zander's suggestion about taking things to the next level that night was such a bad idea.

"I … ." Jared didn't get a chance to finish because a blond ball of energy hurried up to the side of the table and cut him off.

"Well, isn't this cute."

Harper pressed her lips together and internally chastised herself for picking a restaurant her mother regularly frequented. "Mom ... I ... what are you doing here?"

Gloria Harlow smoothed her black miniskirt down and graced her daughter with a long-suffering look. "I'm on a date. What are you doing here?"

Harper swallowed hard. "I'm ... on a date, too."

"So I noticed," Gloria said, swiveling and fixing a bright smile on her face as she looked Jared up and down. "I'm Gloria Harlow. I'm so pleased to meet you." She extended her hand.

Jared stood and shook her hand, fighting the mad urge to laugh as he stood toe-to-toe with Harper's mother. She obviously didn't remember him. "We've actually met before."

Harper mimed zipping her lips, but it was too late.

Gloria knit her eyebrows together. "I don't think that's possible," she said. "I would remember meeting you."

Jared sat back down and leaned back in his chair, stretching his long legs out in front of him as he decided how to answer. "It was a few weeks ago at the police station," he said. "You came in screaming for me to release Harper because you were under the impression that I arrested her."

Gloria faltered. "Oh."

"Mom ... ." Harper was desperate to keep her mother from causing a scene.

Gloria glanced down at Harper. "You're dating the man who arrested you?"

"He didn't arrest me."

"I didn't arrest her," Jared agreed.

"It would be hotter if you had," Gloria shot back, nonplussed. "Well, you're very attractive and I approve. As long as you don't arrest my daughter again, I think we'll get along just fine."

"Mother, you're embarrassing me," Harper gritted out, causing Jared to smirk. He found both of Harper's parents entertaining. Harper was another story. Since her parents were mired in the world's longest divorce – recent arguments turning to who would get the color printer and toner cartridges – she was hoping her mother's

87

current dating trend would keep her out of her hair. Apparently she wasn't that lucky.

"You'll live," Gloria said. "We need to set up a time for brunch so you can catch me up on your life. Apparently I've been missing quite a few things I should know about."

"Who are you out with, Mom?" Harper asked, turning the conversation around. "Have I met this one?"

"I'm dating Ted Gardner."

Harper made a face. "That old guy who has a gray ponytail and rides around on a Harley? You're dating him?"

Jared's shoulders shook with silent laughter as he tried to cover his mouth.

"I'll have you know he's a very generous lover," Gloria replied, causing Harper to make a disgusted sound in the back of her throat. "Jared, it's been a pleasure meeting you. We'll have to set up a brunch so we can get to know one another."

"I would enjoy that," Jared said, and he actually meant it.

"Harper, I'll give you a call this weekend," Gloria said. "We have a few things to discuss."

"I can't wait."

TWELVE

Other than the front porch light, Harper's house was dark when Jared pulled to a stop in front of it several hours later.

All of the nerves the duo put aside during their date came roaring back as a new problem arose.

"Well ... thank you for a wonderful time," Harper said, turning in the passenger seat and fixing Jared with a small smile. "Other than my mother showing up, it was perfect."

"It was perfect even with your mother showing up. She's kind of funny."

"You should try living with her for eighteen years," Harper countered. "It's not so funny then."

"She's good for you. She keeps you on your toes."

"That's one way of looking at it." Harper bit her lip. She was at a loss for what else to talk about. She desperately wanted Jared to kiss her again, but there was no way she was going to make the first move ... or ask him to do it for her. "Well, I guess I should get inside."

"I'll walk you," Jared said, pocketing the keys and hopping out of his truck. He hurried to Harper's side of the vehicle, but she was already halfway out when he arrived. "You're supposed to wait for me to open the door," Jared said, sucking in a steadying breath when

Harper's face moved to within inches of his. Their mouths were so close all one of them would have to do is shift two inches and then .... "I'm supposed to be a gentleman and do that for you."

"I ... ." Harper lost her train of thought.

Jared held out his hand. "I'll walk you to your door."

Harper slipped her hand in his, something sparking between them as they walked up the steps and stopped in front of the door. "I really did have a good time tonight."

Jared turned to her, his handsome face practically glowing under the muted light. "I did, too."

Jared was conflicted. He knew what he wanted to do – Zander's words burrowing into his head the entire night – and yet he didn't want to move so fast Harper would flee in the other direction. He was at a crossroad, and he had no idea what to do.

"I ... ." Harper had no clue what to say. "I guess I'll see you around." She moved her key toward the door, but Jared stilled her with a hand on her forearm. This time when she turned to him she was surprised because he cupped the back of her head with both of his hands. "Are you finally going to make your move?"

The question surprised Jared, causing him to bark out a coarse laugh. "Do you want me to make a move?"

"I have no idea," Harper replied honestly. "My heart is pounding so hard I can't even think straight. I can hear the blood rushing past my ears. I think I might pass out."

"Me, too," Jared whispered, lowering his mouth to Harper's and pressing a soft kiss to her lips. She sank into it, cuddling closer as he held her steady. The kiss went on for what seemed like an eternity, neither one of them wanting to be the first to break it. Finally, Jared moved his head back slightly and met her clear blue eyes with a smoldering look. "You're amazing."

Harper made up her mind on the spot. "Do you want to come inside?"

Jared smiled. "I don't think I could force myself to leave even if I tried."

.   .   .

HARPER WOKE TO AN UNFAMILIAR FEELING: warmth. She shifted her head, pushing her flaxen hair out of her face and met a wall of muscle as she opened her eyes. Jared slumbered beside her, his face placid in sleep. His morning stubble and tousled hair made him look even more appealing ... if that was even possible ... than he had the last time she saw him.

Harper took the opportunity to look him over in the bright light of day. She knew his body would be amazing thanks to the few touches she'd managed through clothing when they were close. Even she wasn't prepared for the chiseled ridges of his chest and arms, though. And his stomach? It looked as if his abs had been drawn on with a marker.

The previous night was a blur, mutual need and instinctive desire taking over both of their bodies as they made their way to Harper's bedroom. Their clothes hit the floor within seconds, and they moved together as if they'd been making love for years instead of it being their first time together. Harper was pretty sure it couldn't possibly get better than it already was ... although she was up to the task of finding out if she got the opportunity.

As if sensing she was awake, Jared shifted and opened his eyes, immediately smiling when he caught sight of her. "Good morning."

"Morning," Harper murmured, embarrassed to be caught looking at him. "Did you sleep okay?"

"I haven't slept that well in ... I can't remember ever sleeping that well," Jared replied, tugging her closer and wrapping his arms around her slender back. "How did you sleep?"

"Like a rock," Harper admitted, chuckling. "I usually wake up a few times every night because ... well, it started after my grandfather came to visit me when I was a kid after he died. I honestly don't think I've slept through a full night since ... until now."

"I guess I tired you out," Jared teased, brushing his lips against Harper's forehead and pressing her head to his chest. "You're so soft and warm. I could get used to this."

Harper stilled, morning jitters overtaking her. "Do you want to get used to this?"

"That's a funny question to ask when we're both naked and snuggled up in your bed," Jared replied. "Since you appear to need an answer, though, then you're going to get one. I definitely want to get used to this."

Harper exhaled heavily, relieved. "Thank you."

Jared laughed. He couldn't help himself. "Are you thanking me for wanting to get used to this, or what we did last night? Before you answer, both of them would be acceptable things to thank me for because one of them makes my ego swell."

That wasn't the only thing swelling. Despite herself, Harper lifted the covers and glanced down to find that Jared appeared to be ready for another round. Jared followed her gaze. "Do you want to thank me again?"

Harper laughed, throwing all of her nerves out the window as she rolled on top of him and slammed her mouth into his. Jared tangled his hands in her hair, marveling at the way her body seemed to meld perfectly against his.

"Can I take that as a yes?" Jared gasped, breaking contact for a moment.

"Yes."

"Good answer."

WELL, WELL, WELL," Zander said, looking up from his mug of coffee when Harper and Jared finally shuffled out of her bedroom and into the kitchen an hour later. "How are my happy … campers?"

Harper made a face. "Don't be a pain."

"That's not a very nice way to treat your best friend in the world," Zander chided. "The best friend, I might add, who cleaned up all your clothes after you left so Jared wouldn't see how panicked you were before your date and also cleared a spot for you two to … camp."

Jared poured two mugs of coffee and handed one to Harper before taking a seat next to Zander at the table. This was something he could get used to, too. Zander was a pain in some respects, but Jared loved watching him interact with Harper. The vibe between the two of them was one of comfort and love. He wasn't sure if he would ever get enough of it.

"How was your date?" Jared asked.

Zander shrugged. "It was fine until the wee hours of the morning. I won't be seeing Mark from the gym again."

"What happened during the wee hours of the morning?"

"Don't ask that question," Harper hissed.

"Why not?" Jared was confused.

"Because you're opening a box of trouble," Harper replied, settling next to Jared. "Zander falls in love once a week and then dumps them as fast as he hooks them."

"How come?"

"Because I'm looking for the perfect man," Zander answered.

"Because he's unbelievably nitpicky," Harper corrected.

"Give me some examples," Jared instructed, enjoying the game.

"Well, he broke up with a garage mechanic because he smelled like gasoline," Harper volunteered.

"It made me nauseous," Zander said.

"He broke up with a waiter because he wore too much cologne."

"And talked with his mouth full of food," Zander added.

"Then there was that guy who works at the county park," Harper said, smiling at the memory. "You chased him for two weeks and then broke up with him because he had hairy toes."

"They freaked me out," Zander said. "I thought he was wearing hobbit slippers when I woke up the next morning."

"That would freak me out, too," Jared said. "Luckily Harper's feet are cute and dainty."

Zander snorted. "She has huge feet for a woman," he said. "It's good you think they're cute, though. You're stuck with them now."

"I can live with that," Jared said, taking another sip. "So, what was wrong with this guy you went out with last night?"

"I'm glad you asked," Zander sniffed. "My best friend clearly doesn't care about my plight ... even though I went out of my way to make sure she looked fabulous for you last night."

"You did a very good job," Jared said.

"That's obvious since you two left clothes between the living room and bedroom on your way to nirvana," Zander said.

"We did not!" Harper was mortified.

"I found your panties sticking out from underneath your bedroom door, Harp," Zander argued, although the twinkle in his eye told Jared the gregarious man couldn't be happier for his best friend. That was another thing Jared liked about Zander. He took joy in Harper's happiness.

"You're making that up," Harper protested.

"Your panties are in the hamper," Zander snapped. "We'll go shopping for sexier ones in the next few days. Poor Jared deserves some options if he's going to have to put up with that bedhead of yours on a regular basis."

Harper instinctively reached for her hair to smooth it, but Jared caught her hand with his and pressed a kiss to her palm instead.

"Your hair looks fine," he said. "I like it that way. It makes me take pride in a job well done."

"You're cheeky," Zander said.

"Go back to your date," Jared instructed, adoration washing over him when he saw Harper try to catch a glimpse of her reflection in the toaster. She was too cute for words. "What did this guy do that was so wrong?"

"Well, it's tragic really," Zander answered. "We were having a perfectly nice interlude and then … well … he took off his shirt."

"Did he have boobs or something?"

"Worse."

"What's wrong with boobs?" Harper asked. "I have them. I kind of like them."

"Yours are great," Jared agreed, squeezing her hand when she blushed. "I don't think Zander likes them, though."

"That's where you're wrong," Harper corrected. "He's obsessed with mine. He won't touch them, though."

Jared frowned. "Why would he touch them?"

"I'm gay," Zander explained. "That's allowed. I still can't touch her boobs. If they belonged to someone else I would be all over them. We're too close. It feels like incest."

"That's good to know," Jared said cautiously. "It's probably going to give me nightmares, but go back to your story. I'm dying to know what was wrong with your date that you only found out when he took his shirt off."

Zander leaned over the table, his expression serious. "He's got an outie."

"A what?"

Harper giggled. "Seriously? Gross."

"I'm missing something," Jared said. "What's an outie?"

Zander lifted his T-shirt and pointed to his belly button.

"Oh," Jared said, realization dawning. "Was it weird?"

"Totally," Zander said. "I tried to ignore it, but it kept rubbing against me and ... well ... I couldn't concentrate. I had to leave."

"Please tell me you didn't sneak out without telling him," Harper chided.

"I'm not your father," Zander replied. "I explained why I had to leave and he was offended. Quite frankly, I think I dodged a bullet. I wouldn't want to date someone that shrill more than once anyway."

"Well, live and learn," Harper said.

"I always do," Zander agreed. "So, tell me all about your date. I heard you ran into your mother."

"How can you possibly know that?"

"She called my mother before she was out of the parking lot and my mother called me first thing this morning," Zander answered. "Tell me every single thing you did – don't get gross, though – and don't leave anything out. We finally get to share date stories again, Harp. I've never been so happy in my entire life."

Harper launched into the retelling, Zander interrupting to ask questions whenever the mood struck.

Jared leaned back in his chair, amused as he sipped his coffee with one hand and held Harper's hand with the other. He definitely could get used to this.

THIRTEEN

"You, my Harp, are practically glowing," Zander said two hours later as he pulled into his regular parking spot at GHI. "You look … happy."

Harper bit her lip, pleased and embarrassed at the same time. "I need to ask you something."

"Yes, I think I'm always going to be this handsome," Zander said without missing a beat.

Harper's smile slipped. "Not that, Mr. Ego," she said. "I need to know what you said to Jared on the front porch yesterday."

Zander was taken aback. "Why?"

"Because I think you said something to him," Harper replied. "Before you get worked up, all he said was that you made him promise to make you dinner and warned him about hurting me."

"I did say those things."

"What else did you say?" Harper knew Zander too well to let him lie to her.

"I told him that you were nervous and to call me if you freaked out," Zander answered, opting for honesty. "I'm not going to feel bad about loving you. I think he's a great guy and you're going to be happy. I wanted him to know that you were nervous, though."

"Did that ... turn him off?"

Zander smirked. "Obviously not since you two ripped each other's clothes off to get at each other."

"That's not what I meant," Harper said, her cheeks burning.

"Harp, he was as nervous and excited as you were," Zander said. "It worked out. I'm not going to apologize for taking care of you. No matter what happens, that's always going to be my job."

"Thank you."

Harper took Zander by surprise when she leaned over and kissed his cheek. Zander pulled her in for a hug before they exited the car and moved toward the office.

"Now that Jared has cleaned out the cobwebs and left for work – with a goofy smile on his face, mind you – you have to tell me how you two actually ended up in bed," Zander instructed. "I was worried he'd wouldn't make a move on the first date. I'm glad I was wrong, but I have to know how it happened."

Harper sighed. "I don't know," she admitted. "We were standing on the front porch feeling like an idiot, and I was going to go inside without so much as a kiss when he kind of grabbed me and kissed me. After ... I just asked him if he wanted to come inside."

"Oh, you're so cute," Zander cooed as he pulled open the door to the office. "I hope this means you two are going to be getting down and dirty on a regular basis now. Jared and his mastery of sex are going to be the best elixir for your skin known to man."

Molly and Eric looked up as Zander and Harper entered, causing Harper's already flushed cheeks to redden.

"Zander!"

Zander wasn't bothered in the least to have an audience. He knew his voice carried and he was fine with it. "Good morning, kids," he said. "How is everyone doing this fine spring day?"

"It's eighty degrees," Eric said, his expression dour.

"Yes, but it's technically still spring for a few more weeks," Zander pointed out. "That's why you have to love a Michigan spring. One day will be eighty and the next will be forty. That's one of the reasons Whisper Cove is so much fun."

"You're in a good mood," Molly said, her eyes bouncing between Harper and Zander. "Did you have a good date last night?"

"Alas, my date had an outie so I had to cut the evening short," Zander replied, sitting in his desk chair and twirling to add flair to the conversation.

"What's an outie?" Eric asked furrowing his brow.

"A belly button that pokes out," Molly explained. "I think they're kind of cute."

"And I think they're weird," Zander said. "It's like one of those timers that pops out when the turkey is done."

"If your date went bad, why are you in such a good mood?" Eric asked.

"Because Harper's date went like a dream," Zander explained. "She and Jared are officially on ... and I believe they climbed on top of each other several times last night – and again this morning – if the noises I heard from her bedroom are any indication."

"I'm going to kill you," Harper hissed, lowering her chin and averting her eyes from Molly's curious stare. She didn't even want to risk a glance at Eric in case his head magically imploded.

"That's great," Molly enthused, her voice climbing an octave. "Oh, I'm so happy for you. I need to know everything." She jumped to her feet and scurried over to Harper's desk. "How does he look naked?"

Harper sat in her chair and purposely swiveled so her back was facing her colleagues. "Um ... he's very attractive."

"He's definitely attractive," Zander agreed. "I couldn't get a very good look at him because he dressed for breakfast, but I did get a glimpse when he snuck into the bathroom this morning. He thought no one was looking. He'll get over that. He could be the cover model on a romance novel."

"Oh, yay!" Molly clapped as she hopped up and down. "I'm so excited. How did this happen?"

"Yeah, how did this happen?" Eric asked, his voice hollow.

Harper pursed her lips, mortified by Molly's excitement and Eric's obvious misery. "It's kind of a long story."

"I'll tell it," Zander offered, twirling in his chair again. "So, Harper and Eric went up to the high school after checking out that house yesterday and ran into Jared. Jared refused to leave until she agreed to go out with him.

"Harper had a meltdown about what to wear, and Jared was a sweating mess when I met him on the front porch, but I sent them on their happy way," he continued. "Apparently they had a wonderful time and hormones overcame them on the front porch. I found a trail of clothes between the living room and Harper's bedroom and they boasted two of the widest smiles I've ever seen over breakfast this morning."

"I'm so happy for you," Molly said, grabbing Harper's hand and forcing her to turn. "How does he look naked? I can tell he's hot just by looking at him, but I need the juicy details."

"I think we should get back to work," Eric said.

"I think Eric's right," Harper agreed, locking gazes with an annoyed Zander. "I ...."

"Don't even think about losing this moment, Harp," Zander chided. "You're happy. Don't let Eric ruin it for you."

"How am I ruining anything?" Eric asked, his eyes widening.

"You know how."

"See, I think I'm the only one worried about Harper in this whole thing," Eric countered. "What happens when this guy upsets her again?"

"That's life," Zander replied. "Nothing is perfect, although Jared seems to be a perfect fit for Harper. He's easygoing and believes in her. Her mother showed up in the middle of dinner and he didn't even flinch when she demanded he have brunch with her."

"Yeah, that was a nightmare," Harper intoned.

"Oh, no," Molly said, giggling. "You know that means your dad is going to want to meet him, too, right?"

"My dad has already met him and likes him."

"He'll want a brunch, though," Zander said. "If your mother gets something he wants it, too. He can't help himself. Where did they land on who gets the printer and cartridges, by the way?"

"They're still haggling."

"I can't believe you guys are so cavalier about this," Eric said, pushing himself to a standing position. "Two days ago we were plotting this guy's death because he left town and didn't bother to call. Now we're supposed to be excited because he took Harper out on a date ... and apparently took advantage of her when it was over?"

"He didn't take advantage of me," Harper argued. "He ... ."

"That's enough," Zander snapped. "Everyone in this room knows why you're being such a pill. Harper knows it. Your little crush on her hasn't escaped her attention. You're not that smooth."

"Zander, don't," Harper warned.

"I don't have a crush on Harper." Eric was shrill. "I ... that's ... I can't believe you said that!"

"Zander is right," Molly said. "Everyone knows you have a crush on Harper. She's too nice to shoot you down, though."

"You need to shut up!" Eric threatened, wagging a finger in Molly's face. "This has nothing to do with you."

Harper felt as if she was drowning in a sea of negativity, and after her wonderful night and blissful morning, that was the last thing she wanted. She hauled herself to a standing position, shaking her head as everyone continued to battle about her love life, and moved toward the door.

"Harp, where are you going?" Zander asked her retreating back.

"I'm not letting you guys ruin this for me," Harper said. "Zander is right. I'm happy. I want to stay happy. That's why I'm going for a walk."

"No one is trying to ruin anything for you," Eric said.

"You are," Zander shot back, returning to the argument.

"I'll see you guys later," Harper said, breezing through the door. There was no way she was going to be able to put up with this on a regular basis. Something was going to have to shift in that office. She had no idea what, though.

HARPER AIMLESSLY WANDERED the streets for twenty minutes, her mind busy. Memories of the previous evening – every soft touch and kiss – bombarded her as she tried to push Eric's sad face out of her mind. She was going to have to sit him down and force some realities on him. There was no doubt about that. She wasn't good with emotional stuff and uncomfortable conversations, and the idea made her sick to her stomach.

Before she realized what was happening, Harper found herself back at the park. It was empty. Only a ghoul wanted to hang out in a park where a boy died – and those people waited until it was dark to cut down on the possibility of people seeing them.

The police tape remained, although dragging low in some places, and Harper circled it as she tried to force her mind from memories of Jared. Derek Thompson was murdered. She was convinced of that. There could be no other reason for him to haunt his death spot. Now … if he would only talk to her.

"I see you're back," Derek said, popping into view.

"Ask and you shall receive," Harper muttered.

"What?"

"Nothing." Harper shook her head and focused on Derek. "I see you're back, too. How are you?"

"I'm dead. How are you?"

Teenagers are a pain in life and death apparently, Harper internally mused. She didn't even like herself as a teenager. It was getting harder and harder to pretend Derek wasn't a snot. "I saw your girlfriend yesterday," she said, changing tactics.

Derek snorted. "Oh, man. You saw Lexie? I'll bet she's milking this thing to her advantage every chance she gets."

That was a cynical way to talk about your girlfriend, Harper internally mused. "She's … in mourning." Harper didn't want to malign the girl in case she really was upset. The problem was, Harper couldn't identify one real emotion from Lexie during their previous exchange. "Some of your friends … Brandon, Dylan, and David, to be exact … were with her. They were consoling her."

"The only thing Brandon is trying to console is Lexie's hoo-ha."

Harper hadn't heard that term in … well, she wasn't sure she'd ever heard that term. "Her … hoo-ha?"

"You know, her ... hoo-ha," Derek said.

If he was trying to clarify something, he was doing a rotten job. Still, Harper knew what he was referring to. "Did Lexie and Brandon have a thing?"

"Lexie doesn't have a thing with anyone," Derek countered. "She was my girlfriend, but that's only because I'm popular and she likes attention. Brandon doesn't have a shot because he's not really popular and now she's going to be getting all the attention she could ever want because I'm dead."

"That's kind of the feeling I got from her, too," Harper admitted. "Everyone was up at the school yesterday for some summer classes. It's weird to me that you guys get out so early and then immediately have to go to summer school. I know the school year is truncated here because of old farming traditions, but it seems weird to me that summer school is already in session."

"I never had to do that," Derek countered. "Lexie only has to do it because I refused to do her algebra. She was looking for a boyfriend who was smart in math, but she had no idea my mother did my algebra for me. She's an accountant. It was easy for her."

Harper frowned. She knew Derek's mother and had no idea the woman could be so easily swayed. "That's not exactly helping you."

"When am I ever going to need algebra?"

"I ... ." Harper didn't have an answer because she'd never once used algebra since graduating from high school. She decided to refocus Derek's attention on something important. "Have you remembered anything about your death?"

Derek shrugged. "It's weird," he said after a moment. "I keep having flashes of stuff, but they could be from any time. One minute I'll be thinking of something I did as a kid and the next minute I'll be at a party where I had a lot of fun ... and got laid. I'm going to miss sex the most I think."

Harper bit her tongue to keep a harsh retort at bay. "What about the night you died?" she pressed. "Try to walk me through what happened."

"That's still fuzzy," Derek said. "I remember being in my bedroom and getting a call from David. He said everyone was meeting in the park to hang out and have a few beers. I don't remember leaving the house and I don't remember arriving here. I must have, though, right?"

Harper knit her eyebrows together. "They said they didn't see you the night you died. They said they weren't at the park. Are you sure David called you?"

"Yeah. Why would they say they weren't here? David was already on his way when he called."

"I don't know."

Derek's face was unreadable. "Maybe I'm confusing the nights," he said finally. "I don't think I am, though."

"Keep trying to remember," Harper instructed. "If you think you were coming here, odds are you were. If you're blocking what happened to you, it's probably because you don't want to remember."

"Will I ever remember?"

"I don't know," Harper said, opting for honesty. "It's different for every ghost."

"I always thought you and Zander were playing a game when you said that you could see ghosts," Derek said. "I guess I was wrong, huh?"

"Zander can't see ghosts," Harper clarified. "He merely has faith that I can."

"You can, though," Derek said. "You're the only one who can see me. Do you know how awful it is to go to my house and see my parents shutting down and not be able to talk to them?"

"I'm sure that's rough," Harper replied, her heart going out to the boy. He might be brash and insensitive, but he was still a teenager struggling with the loss of his own life. He would never get to do the things he wanted to do. He would never get married and have children of his own. He would never mature beyond his current age. That had to be wearing on him. "You can only do what you can do. Try to remember what happened to you that night. It's important."

"Why?"

"Because if someone killed you – and I believe that's what

happened – then they might kill again," Harper said. "It's too late to save you, although when you're ready, I can help you move on to a better place. It's not too late to save someone else."

"I never thought about that," Derek said. "Okay. I'll do my best."

"That's all you can do."

FOURTEEN

"Okay, I've got the final autopsy results back and there's some interesting stuff in here," Jared said, sitting in his desk chair and turning so he was facing Mel as he perused the information.

Mel looked his partner up and down with a studied eye. "Why do you look different?"

Jared tore his attention away from the file and focused on his partner. "What do you mean?"

"You look different," Mel said. "You're ... different. I don't know how to explain it. Did something happen?"

A lot happened, but there was no way Jared was going to talk to Mel about it. He knew the older cop would find out on his own – Zander had loose lips – but he wasn't the kiss-and-tell type. Well, he'd already told Mel about kissing Harper, so that wasn't exactly true. He wasn't the share-the-sex-details type, though. He wouldn't disrespect Harper in that manner.

"Nothing happened," Jared answered, even though he was chalking the previous evening up as one of the best nights of his life. "Do you want to talk about Derek now, or do you want to keep harping on how I look different?"

Mel shrugged. "Have it your way," he said. "I'll figure it out eventually."

"I'm sure you will," Jared said, returning his attention to the file. "So, the preliminary toxicology reports show that Derek was drinking before his death."

Mel stiffened. "I ... are you sure?"

"He had a blood alcohol content level of .18. He was drunk." Jared softened his voice, but there was no way he could ease the blow. Mel wanted to believe Derek was some misbegotten angel brutally ripped out of his life. While drinking teenagers wasn't a new thing – and it certainly didn't make Derek a bad kid – Mel and Jared had to look at all of the facts if they wanted to solve the case.

"I guess I shouldn't be surprised," Mel said, rubbing the back of his neck. "That place has always been a party spot. There wasn't anything else in his system, was there?"

"That will come with the full toxicology results," Jared replied. "We don't know. If it's any consolation, I have a feeling we won't find anything worse than pot in his system because he was an athlete. He had to be drug tested, and if he was hitting the harder stuff someone probably would've found out before now."

"That's not going to make this easier on his parents," Mel pointed out.

"I don't think anything is going to make this easier on his parents," Jared said. "The blow to his head was quick and efficient. He died within minutes, and probably lost consciousness the moment he was struck. The medical examiner still can't say with any certainty that he was hit with something, but since no blood was found on the merry-go-round and that was the only thing hard enough to kill him, he's ruling it a homicide."

"I don't think that surprises either of us," Mel said. "Where do you think we should focus first?"

"I want to look at the kids harder," Jared said. "I didn't get the feeling that Lexie was anything but disingenuous while we were there, and the other kids seemed ... furtive."

"Furtive?"

"That's the best way I can describe it," Jared explained. "They kept trying to focus the conversation on Harper because they didn't want us asking probing questions about Derek. I can't be the only one who noticed that."

"Well, it was hard to notice anything with all the hormones flying around, but I think you're right," Mel said. "I'll get in touch with Jim and see if he can put a definitive list of Derek's friends together. Tomorrow we'll start questioning them alone. It's harder for them to hide when they're not in a group."

"I agree," Jared said. "I ... ." He broke off when he saw the door to a small department open, allowing Harper entrance. His heart flipped at the sight of her. Their gazes locked across the expanse, and she took a tentative step in his direction. "Hey."

Mel glanced over his shoulder and scowled when he saw what entranced his partner. "Hello, Harper. Are you here on a social call or official business?"

Harper smiled shyly as she moved closer, forcing her eyes from Jared. "Official business."

Jared couldn't help but be a little disappointed. He realized that made him something of a lovesick puppy, but he couldn't muster the energy to care. "What have you been doing today?"

"Well, I stopped in at the office, but things were kind of ... unproductive ... there," Harper answered. "Then I took a walk and ran into Derek at the park."

Mel straightened, his interest piqued. "I'm not sure I believe you see ghosts, just for the record, but out of curiosity, did Derek say anything?"

"He still doesn't remember how he died," Harper said, nervously taking the chair next to Jared when he gestured toward it. "He did say something interesting, though, and I thought you guys should know about it."

Mel arched an eyebrow. "Are you purposely dragging this out so you can stare at Jared for a few minutes longer?"

"No," Harper said, snapping her head around and blushing furiously. "I ... sorry ... I ... ."

"Leave her alone," Jared instructed. "There's no reason to be mean to her just because you're upset about the toxicology report."

"I'm not being mean to her," Mel countered. "I've known her since she was this high." He gestured to his knee for emphasis. "She knows I love her. Not all of us turn into mush when she walks into a room, though."

Jared rolled his eyes. "What did Derek say?"

"He said he remembers getting a call from David the night he was killed," Harper replied. "He said they wanted him to go to the park because they were going to hang out. I personally think 'hang out' is code for party, but he didn't really expand on that."

"He was drunk when he died," Jared informed her. "We just got the toxicology report. I'm guessing he made it there. It's funny none of the kids mentioned seeing him, though."

"No, they all specifically said they didn't see him," Harper pointed out. "I don't know if that means they're guilty or not, but I think they're hiding something. Lexie is definitely hiding something."

"Yeah, she's full of herself," Jared said. "Jim said she thinks she's going to get through life on her looks and that high school popularity means something in the real world. I think she's got a rude awakening in her future."

"Derek also said that he expected Lexie to be playing on everyone's emotions so she could be the center of attention and he made an offhand comment about Brandon wanting to see her hoo-ha."

Jared smiled. He couldn't help it. Harper was so cute when she said the word "hoo-ha" he almost grabbed her and kissed her right there. If Mel was otherwise engaged he would have his hands on her without question. "Hoo-ha?"

"That's what he called it," Harper clarified. "He also said he thought he was going to miss sex the most."

"Ugh," Mel said, making a face. "Don't tell me things like that."

"I'm sorry. I thought you would want all of the information," Harper said. "I didn't get the feeling Derek was particularly fond of Lexie. He didn't talk about her as if he cared about her. It was more ...

perfunctory. Like he needed a girlfriend and knew she would do for the time being."

"How did you leave things?" Jared asked.

"He's going to try remembering what happened and I told him I would be around to listen if he got any information."

"I don't like this," Mel said, getting to his feet. "Why would those kids lie unless they did something to Derek?"

"Don't jump to conclusions," Jared said, his fingers moving to Harper's cheek as if they had a mind of their own. He brushed his thumb over her soft skin and smiled. "Just because they're hiding something, that doesn't mean they're automatically murderers. Derek might've fallen someplace else and they moved his body because they panicked or something. We just don't know yet."

"I guess that's a possibility," Mel said, turning back. "I ... oh, good grief. Are you petting her in the middle of our office?"

Jared snatched his hand back, regaining his senses. He couldn't stop himself from touching Harper and now he felt like a teenager about to be scolded by his father. "I ... um ... what were we talking about?"

Harper cleared her throat. "I think something had to happen to cause Derek to stay behind," she said. "I can only think of a handful of ghosts I've come across who died by accident. Most of them were killed and their souls clung to this world so they could make sure that someone paid for their murder."

"We can't make a case on your ghost logic, Harper," Mel said. "I don't mean to be rude, but if we tell anyone anything you just said we'll be laughed out of court."

"I'm not suggesting that," Harper shot back. "I'm just saying that I believe he was murdered ... or at least something utterly tragic happened that night that he can't wrap his head around yet."

Mel held up his hands in a placating manner. "I'm sorry if I offended you."

"I'm not offended."

Mel pressed the heel of his hand to his forehead, narrowing his eyes as he watched Jared and Harper silently flirty. "Oh, holy hell! I know why you look different."

Jared wrenched his gaze away from Harper. "What do you mean?"

"You two finally played tickle the pickle last night and now you're more infatuated with one another than you were yesterday," Mel said. "I'm such an idiot. It was written all over your face when you walked in here this morning."

"Tickle the pickle?" Jared barked out a laugh. "Is that some old saying I've never heard before?"

"Well, you're not denying it, so it must be true," Mel said. "Does Zander know? He can't. If he knew he would've called his mother and she would be deluging me with calls to find out if Jared is good enough for Harper."

Harper bit her lip. "I ... ."

"Zander knows," Jared replied matter-of-factly. "We all had breakfast together this morning. Perhaps your family gossip mill is broken."

Mel's cell phone buzzed on top of his desk and he glanced down. "Or perhaps Zander is merely late spreading the gossip," he said. "This is my sister now. I've got twenty bucks that says she's about to tell me you two got horizontal last night." Mel picked up the phone and pressed it to his ear. "Now isn't a good time to ... ." He broke off, his face coloring. "You don't say? Harper has a new boyfriend? I'm shocked."

Mel took his conversation to the other side of the room, conveniently leaving Jared and Harper to continue with their flirt fest.

"You look pretty," Jared said. "I'm sorry I had to rush out after breakfast. I had no idea how late it was and I needed to run home so I could change my clothes."

"It's okay," Harper offered. "I understand. The world doesn't stop just because ... ."

"I shared my pickle with you?" Jared suggested, grinning.

"I don't think I like that saying."

"It's an odd one," Jared agreed, running his fingertips over Harper's hand. "I don't think we're going to be late tonight. We're going to start pulling those kids in individually for questioning tomorrow. I was thinking that I would pick up steaks, potatoes, and wine before going to your place tonight."

Harper was pleasantly surprised by the suggestion. "You want to see me again tonight?"

"Yeah, we're going to have a talk about why you're surprised by that later," Jared said, keeping his voice low. "As far as I'm concerned, I always want to see you. I need to make Zander his dinner before he has a meltdown."

"He's your biggest fan right now," Harper said. "I think he'd probably let you out of the dinner promise if you don't want to cook."

"I like to grill," Jared countered. "Why is Zander my biggest fan? Shouldn't you be my biggest fan?"

"I'm trying to be cool so you don't think I'm a spaz," Harper explained. "If I say I'm your biggest fan my mind automatically goes to giggling girls at a boy band concert. That's a freaky thought."

"If you want to scream and clap for me, I'll take it as a compliment," Jared whispered, pressing a soft kiss to her lips before risking a glance in Mel's direction and finding his partner glaring at him. "We're going to have to watch ourselves around Mel. He doesn't seem to have much of a sense of humor regarding all of this."

"I'm sure we'll figure something out," Harper said. She was trying to rein in her smile ... and failing miserably. "If you're really cooking dinner for us, you should stop by your place and grab more clothes. I'm going to want to reward you after, and this way you won't have to rush out again tomorrow morning."

"You're getting bolder," Jared said. "I like that. That's a very good idea. What else should I bring for dinner? Do you like vegetables?"

"Just don't bring something phallic," Harper suggested. "I'm not going to be able to touch pickles for a week as it is."

Jared chuckled. "You're so cute."

"You sound like Zander."

"I'm going to take that as a compliment, even though it makes me marginally uncomfortable," Jared said. "Now that he's used the word 'incest' in conjunction with you, I don't want to be compared to him."

"You have a dirty mind."

"Only where you're concerned," Jared said, giving in and kissing her again.

"All right, we need to come up with some ground rules," Mel said, disconnecting his phone and tossing it on his desk as he fixed Harper and Jared with a hard look. "I think it's great you two are all over each other. I don't want to see it, though."

"I won't stop by again," Harper said, pushing herself up from the chair.

"That's not fair," Jared protested. "She might have an actual tip for us. You can't ban her."

"I'm not banning her," Mel said. "I cannot watch another display like this, though. Harper, when you come to the office you have to stand at least five feet away from Jared. That's the new rule."

Jared was incensed. "No way."

"It's fine," Harper said, patting his arm. "It will make things more fun. It will be like a really weird game."

"Yes, but I want to win this game," Jared said. "Don't worry about it. I'll talk to him. I'll see you for dinner in a few hours."

"I can't wait."

"Me either." Jared shot a challenging look in Mel's direction before grabbing Harper's chin and planting another kiss on her. "I'll see you soon."

FIFTEEN

"I think you brought enough food to feed five more people," Harper said shortly after six, taking one of the grocery bags from Jared and leading him through the house. "How much are you planning on making?"

"I might have gone overboard," Jared conceded, dropping his duffel bag on the floor of the kitchen and kicking it into the corner so no one would trip over it. "I wanted to make sure Zander was happy with his meal."

Zander sat at the kitchen table with an open Victoria's Secret catalog, his eyes briefly traveling to Jared's bag before returning to his previous task. "I see you thought ahead this time," he said. "Picking up clothes so you can spend the night and not race out the next morning is a good move."

"It was my idea," Harper said, digging into one of the grocery bags and pulling out a bottle of wine. She frowned when she read the label. "Zander isn't going to drink this."

Jared made a face as he collected the wine from her. "That is not for drinking, my dear," he said, brushing a quick kiss against Harper's cheek for good measure before returning to his groceries. "This is for marinating the steaks. It's cooking wine."

"If you're marinating the steaks, that means I'm not going to get dinner until at least eight and I'm starving," Zander complained, taking a pen to mark something on one of the catalog pages. "This dinner already sounds like a disaster."

"I'm making you stuffed mushrooms as an appetizer," Jared countered. "Chill out. I did bring some real wine if you need something to help you relax."

"I do like stuffed mushrooms," Zander said. "Harper, leave your hunky boyfriend to his cooking and come over here and help me pick you out some passable lingerie."

Harper froze, her gaze flitting to Jared for a moment. She looked like a deer caught in headlights. "I ... ."

Jared chuckled. "Where would I find mixing bowls?"

"Under the cupboard next to the sink," Zander replied, not looking up. "I think you're too pale for red, Harp. It doesn't go with your coloring for some reason. I think we're better going with blues, purples, and blacks for you."

"Put that catalog away, Zander," Harper hissed. "You can't do stuff like that in front of Jared. It's ... embarrassing."

"He's already seen you naked," Zander shot back. "This stuff is for him as much as it is for you, by the way. I'm sure he's fine with it."

Harper shot Jared a "help me" look.

"Oh, you're on your own," Jared said. "This conversation has 'fun' written all over it. There's a dirty quality about a man looking at a lingerie catalog with my girlfriend while I'm in the same room, and yet it's also mundane in a weird way. Go over there and shop with your friend. I'll handle dinner."

"Listen to him, Harp," Zander said, patting the seat next to him. He held up the catalog as she closed the distance. "What do you think about this one? You're not exactly what I would call well endowed, but you have enough to fake it if you have a bra like this."

"I'm going to kill you," Harper threatened, glaring at the photograph Zander held up. "I am not wearing that. I'd look like a hooker."

"I'm not asking you to wear it in public," Zander scoffed. "It's for Jared's private viewing. Although, I read an article once that said if women feel like they're wearing pretty undergarments they carry themselves better in the outside world. People make fun of you sometimes. I'll bet that's because you wear cotton panties too often."

Jared poured the bottle of cooking wine over the steaks and covered them with plastic wrap before shoving them into the refrigerator. He then poured three glasses of a more expensive wine and delivered them to the table before gathering his stuffed mushroom ingredients and joining Zander and Harper. He wanted to be part of the fun, too.

"That's pretty," Jared said, separating the mushroom heads from the stems. "I think everything you already have is fine, though."

"See," Harper said, sipping her wine.

"Don't encourage her," Zander chided. "I'm trying to get her to experiment."

"You told me that you were experimenting when you tried to get Brad Locksley to kiss you when we were in middle school," Harper reminded him. "Your experiments don't usually end well."

"Yes, well, I still maintain he was gay and he just didn't know it," Zander said. "It's just like Jim Stone. I think he's gay, too. That's why he didn't like me in high school. He was a closeted self-loather."

Jared stirred at the words. "I met him yesterday," he said. "He seemed like a nice enough guy, although he did mention having a feud with the two of you. What's the deal with that?"

"It's not a feud," Harper countered. "He's a jackass."

Zander patted Harper's arm before flipping the catalog page. "Jim and Harper are mortal enemies," he supplied. "She's threatened to set him on fire more times than I can count."

"She did it yesterday," Jared said. "When I first met Jim I wasn't sure if I was going to like him because Mel said he had a crush on Harper. Then I found out Harper hated him and I felt better. He seems to genuinely care about the kids, and he mentioned something happening between the three of you in high school."

"It doesn't matter," Harper said, pushing her bottom lip out as she pointed at something in the catalog. "That's pretty."

Jared realized that the story was must be bad if she was willing to indulge Zander and shop for lingerie. "You don't have to tell me," Jared said. "It's okay."

"It's not that bad," Zander said, marking the item Harper liked with his pen. "It's just … when you're the only gay kid in a town the size of Whisper Cove, well, things can get uncomfortable. I was fairly popular in high school – especially with the girls – but some of the boys were uncomfortable around me."

"Because they were jackasses," Harper interjected.

Jared hadn't seen Harper this wound up since the night he almost arrested her. He was intrigued.

"Jim was on the football team with a bunch of other kids, including Dominic Walker," Zander explained. "Dominic's father was on the township council and I guess Dominic asked him to make it so I couldn't shower in the boys' locker room after gym class because it made the other guys uncomfortable."

Harper made a growling sound in the back of her throat as Jared frowned.

"They can't do that," Jared argued. "That's against the law."

"Whisper Cove is tiny," Zander said. "My parents and Mel took up the fight, and it got so big it was actually added to the agenda at one of the town meetings."

Jared's heart sank. "You've got to be kidding me."

Zander shook his head. "Everyone got up in front of the township board and Dominic said that he was worried I was checking him out and he felt sexually harassed."

"Like anyone would want to sexually harass his fat ass," Harper seethed.

"I'm worried you have somehow suddenly developed Tourette's," Jared said, reaching over and squeezing Harper's hand to comfort her. "We don't have to talk about this."

"Let's get it out of the way now," Zander countered. "The odds of Harper threatening to set Jim Stone on fire again are pretty good. She does it whenever she runs into him."

Jared nodded, his eyes locking onto Zander's momentarily before he turned back to his mushrooms. "I don't understand how this could've been brought up at a township meeting. It's ludicrous."

"Well, it was," Zander said. "The school officials had no balls and I was told I either had to use the girls' locker room by myself after gym class or pick another elective class."

"Did Jim say anything about you at the meeting?" Jared asked. "How does he play into all of this, other than being this Dominic kid's friend, I mean?"

"All of the guys said they were uncomfortable with me being around them," Zander answered. "You could tell most of them were following a script written by Dominic. Jim ... added a little something to his statement."

"What?"

Zander opened his mouth, and for the first time Jared realized that the man didn't know what to say.

"He said that Zander tried to force him to kiss him one day in the locker room," Harper answered for her best friend. "He lied to everyone and said Zander was a deviant."

"I can't believe he did that."

"Well, believe it," Harper said. "That's your buddy."

"Hey, I'm not making excuses for him," Jared countered. "I spent exactly ten minutes with the man. He expressed regret about what he did. I had no idea what that was, though. I'm sorry this happened ... to both of you."

"My mother wanted to take the school and the township board to court," Zander explained, regaining his composure. "Mel was on her side even though Dominic's father made noise about getting him fired from the department. I didn't want that. I didn't want to be anyone's symbol."

"What did you do?" Jared asked.

"I took home economics," Zander said, smiling at the memory and alleviating some of the tension in the room. "It was the best decision I ever made. I learned how to sew and the women loved my chocolate chip cookies. Isn't that right, Harp?"

Harper graced Zander with a smile. "You're the only reason I passed that class."

"Yes, you've always been horrible in the kitchen," Zander said, leaning forward and rubbing his nose against Harper's to get her to ease up the rest of the way. "It all worked out in the end."

"Has Jim ever apologized to you?" Jared asked. "He made it sound as if he's tried, but Harper always stops him and that she's being unreasonable."

"If you want to know the truth about that whole thing, I think Jim has always had a crush on Harper that he can't quite seem to shake," Zander explained. "He always tried to get close to her ... hang out with her ... get her to go to a movie and stuff. She preferred hanging out with me and he was jealous."

"Like I would ever hang out with him," Harper huffed. "I already had the best friend in the world. I didn't need the likes of him."

"After the scene at the township hall, Jim asked Harper out," Zander said. "She ... had a very loud reaction."

"I might have heard something about that," Jared snickered. "What did she do?"

"She kicked him in the balls and told him now she was sexually harassing him and asked him how it felt," Zander replied. "She was hauled into the principal's office and suspended for an entire week. Well, actually she was offered the chance to apologize first and she refused."

"My little vigilante," Jared teased. "Did you get in trouble with your parents?"

"My parents never agreed about anything when I was a kid," Harper said. "They agreed that I was right for doing what I did that day, though. My punishment was to go shopping and eat ice cream every day for a week. Zander faked sick in a show of solidarity and we watched oodles of soap operas and gossiped about how much we hated everyone else."

"That sounds like fun," Jared said. "Whatever happened to that Dominic kid?"

"He moved after graduation and never came back," Harper replied. "His father is still on the town council."

"Well, I can't wait to meet him," Jared said, shaking himself out of his sad reverie. "Who wants to help me make stuffed mushrooms?"

"We're shopping for lingerie," Zander said. "Cooking is your chore tonight."

THREE HOURS later Harper shut her bedroom door and faced Jared as he sat on the end of her bed.

"Your dinner was delicious," she said. "Zander loves you even more now. You should be proud."

"It was just steak and potatoes," Jared replied, his expression thoughtful.

"Take your clothes off," Harper ordered, impatient. "I've been thinking about you naked all day."

Jared chuckled softly. "I will in a minute. I want to talk to you for a second."

Harper stilled, worry flitting through her stomach. "Is something wrong? Did you change your mind about staying the night?"

"No," Jared replied, making a face. "I'm not going to change my mind about that, so stop imagining things that aren't going to happen. I want to talk to you about the story you told me about Zander."

"Oh." Harper's face fell. "I don't really want to talk about that again. It upsets me."

"I've noticed," Jared said. "I want you to know that I think it's great how you and Zander stand up for one another. I've never seen two people more loyal to each other. It's wonderful."

Harper lifted her chin, surprised. "You don't think I'm horrible for kicking Jim in the balls? Most people think I should've gotten in more trouble for that."

"I think you did the exact right thing," Jared said, patting his lap. "Come here a second."

Harper did as instructed, snuggling close as Jared wrapped his arms around her waist.

"I already thought you were great before I heard that story," Jared said. "Now I think you're ... amazing. Zander is lucky to have you."

"I'm lucky to have him," Harper countered. "People made fun of him for being gay, but they went after me because there were rumors about how odd I was. Zander put up with a lot more than I did."

Jared brushed his lips against Harper's cheek. "Teenagers want to be the same and they abhor anything different," he said. "They're like chickens. They peck anything outside the norm to death.

"When people get older, they realize that being different is the best thing in the world," he continued. "I wouldn't want you to be normal, if that's even the way to phrase that. I wouldn't want you any other way than you already are. You're ... perfect."

Harper pursed her lips as she lifted her flirty eyes. "You're about to get really lucky."

"I have a feeling I already have," Jared said, pushing Harper's hair away from her face. "Don't ever change who you are. Not for anything. Don't let Zander change either. Together you two are ... magical. If other people can't see that, it's their loss."

"Thank you," Harper said, shifting on Jared's lap. "Now I need you to take your shirt off. I'm not done drooling over your chest yet. It got cut short this morning."

Jared pressed a firm kiss to her mouth. "Yes, ma'am. Just for the record ... I like it when you're bossy."

"In that case, you should probably take your pants off, too," Harper ordered. "I want to see that again, too."

"Yup. I definitely like it when you're bossy."

SIXTEEN

"Good morning, Harp."

Jared tightened his arms around Harper's bare back when he felt her stirring the next morning, hoping to keep her close for a few minutes longer because he loved the way her body felt next to his.

Harper lifted her head, her blue eyes surprisingly bright for so early in the morning. "Good morning. You can't call me that."

Jared still, surprised. "What? Harp? That's what Zander calls you sometimes."

"I know. That's why you can't call me that," Harper said, kissing Jared's strong chin. "He'll have a fit. That's his nickname for me and if anyone tries to use it – including my mother – he'll yell."

Jared frowned as he smoothed Harper's honey-colored hair away from her face. "I want something to call you."

"Why?"

"I have no idea," Jared admitted. "I just do. If I can't call you Harp, what can I call you?"

"Um … I have no idea," Harper said. "I've never been faced with this dilemma before. You could call me … honey."

"No. That's too generic."

"Sweetie?"

"Also too generic."

"I don't know what to tell you," Harper said. "I'm going to call you Jared. I don't think you're the nickname sort."

"Do you have a nickname for Zander?"

"Is this a competition?" Harper challenged. "If so, I'm going to need coffee before we start playing this game."

"Do you have a nickname for Zander?" Jared pressed. "I'm going to feel left out if he has a nickname and I don't."

"Not really," Harper said, sighing as she gave in. "Sometimes I guess I call him Zand, but that's very rare. Although, when we were in middle school he tried to get me to start calling him 'Zan the man.' I have no idea why, but it didn't catch on."

Jared snickered as he traced a lazy pattern across Harper's naked shoulder. "I'm going to come up with something that only I can call you."

"I have no idea why this is so important to you, but go nuts," Harper said, burrowing her face in the hollow between Jared's neck and chest. "You're so warm. I don't ever want to get out of this bed."

"That's going to make paying the bills rough, but I'm willing to give it a try."

"I slept the whole night again," Harper mused. "That's two nights in a row. I think you might be magic."

"Well, I already know you're magic," Jared said. "What are you doing today, my magical wonder?"

"I'm not sure," Harper replied. "I left the office early yesterday because Eric and Zander were fighting and I have no idea if we got anything new."

"Why were Zander and Eric fighting?"

"Take one guess."

Jared arched an eyebrow. "Me?"

"Zander went to great pains to make sure everyone knew what happened between us," Harper explained. "He was trying to send a message to Eric because I can't seem to make myself be mean to him."

"I'll do it for you."

Harper pinched Jared's side. "I don't want to be mean to him. He's a nice guy. He's just ... oblivious."

"I don't think he's as oblivious as you want to believe," Jared said. "Still, he's your employee. He's yours to deal with as you see fit. If he makes a move on you, though, I'm going to have to beat him up."

Harper snorted. "Nice. What are you doing today?"

"I'm hauling all of those kids in so I can question them," Jared replied, the real world intruding on their interlude as he sobered. "I'm hitting Lexie first. For some reason I can't help but feel she's important to all of this."

"It's funny," Harper mused. "She wants to be important so badly she can't help herself, and now that she really is all she wants to do is play a game and gather as much sympathy as possible."

"I think I'm going to take a soft touch with her," Jared said. "She likes it when people – men especially – pay attention to her. Maybe if I start out asking about her she'll be more apt to open up."

"That's a good idea," Harper said, rolling so she was on top of Jared. "Before you go, though, I was hoping you could take a soft touch with me."

"That's the best offer I've had all morning."

"HOW WAS YOUR NIGHT?" Mel asked two hours later, leaning against the hallway wall in the police station and watching through the window as Lexie Studebaker shifted uncomfortably in her chair in the nearby office. They were trying to make her sweat before entering.

"It was good," Jared replied, smiling.

"Don't be filthy."

"I'm not being filthy," Jared countered. "We all had dinner together and hung out, and then Harper and I ... went to sleep."

"Better," Mel said. "How is Zander taking you moving in on his Harper turf?"

"He seems fine," Jared answered. "I'm not entirely convinced there's not going to be a territorial dispute at some point, but for now he seems genuinely happy for Harper and ready to stand back and let her enjoy herself."

"Zander loves Harper and he'll do whatever it takes to keep her happy," Mel said. "He's also the type to get his panties in a wad when he feels like it, so watch out for that. Even if he does pick a fight with you, though, he would never purposely upset Harper ... well, except when he's trying to pick a fight with her because those two enjoy sniping at each other from time to time."

"I think they're cute," Jared said. "Although, last night things did get a little deep there for a few minutes. Zander told me what happened between Jim Stone and him."

Mel scowled. "That whole thing was a big pile of crap," he said. "I wanted to take it all the way down the line, but Zander refused. He didn't want everyone fighting for him and risking themselves in the process. That kid is a pain in the ass when he wants to be, but he has a good heart."

"He has a great heart," Jared agreed. "How come you're friendly with Jim after what he did?"

"Jim is sorry for what happened back then," Mel said. "He admits things got out of hand and he felt pressured to back Dominic up. For the record, he's the only reason Harper didn't get in a mess of trouble for kicking him in the balls. Once he could breathe again he went straight to the principal and said he provoked her. Harper is lucky she got off as lightly as she did."

"She's not sorry."

"She's definitely not sorry," Mel said. "I don't blame her. She was Zander's rock during that time. He's stood by her through a mess of stuff, but no one dared take Harper on back then because she was terrifying."

"It's hard to believe something so cute could be considered terrifying."

"Oh, son, you've got it so bad I'm going to have to quarantine you if this keeps up," Mel warned. "I'm hoping it's just that heady beginning of a relationship phase you're going through, because if this goes on for more than a week I'm going to have to kick you in the balls."

"I'll take that under advisement," Jared said, unconsciously shifting his pelvis away from Mel. "Are you ready to question the queen bee?"

"Let's do it."

Mel and Jared let themselves into the office and settled across from Lexie. She looked nervous, although she put on a bright smile for their benefit.

"Am I in some sort of trouble?"

"You're not in any trouble," Jared said, his tone warm and his face open. "We just need some information about Derek."

"We've run into a wall regarding his death and we're trying to get any leads we can," Mel added. Jared and Mel agreed to approach Lexie on her level first to see if they could get her to volunteer anything. If that failed, they were ready to hammer her.

"I miss him so much," Lexie said. "His funeral is tomorrow. Did you know that?"

"His parents told me," Mel replied.

"They said I could sit up front with them because we were in love and they know I'm crushed," Lexie said, making a mournful face that didn't make it all the way to her twinkling eyes.

"That's nice for you," Jared said, swallowing his distaste. "We're really confused, Lexie. We need to know why Derek was in that park the night he died. Have you come up with anything that might help us?"

Lexie shook her head. "I honestly don't know," she said. "We hung out in the park occasionally, most of the time to just share pop and talk, but no one had plans to go that night."

Jared internally rolled his eyes at the "pop" reference. "Well, I just don't know what to make of this. Do you know what to make of this, Mel?"

"I'm stumped," Mel replied, rubbing his chin. "You see, Lexie, the problem we have is that someone told us that you guys were meeting at the park that night. In fact, we know David Martin called Derek and invited him to the park. We have the phone records to prove it."

That was a lie. They were in the process of getting the phone records, but they didn't have actual proof of Derek's statement yet. It didn't matter because they couldn't attribute the statement to a ghost if it came down to it. They agreed to keep things vague in case the kids opted to turn on each other out of fear.

For the first time since he met her Jared saw true emotion move across Lexie's face. It was brief, but for a moment she looked frightened.

"W-what?" Lexie asked.

"Yeah, David called Derek the night he died," Mel verified. "Derek left a few minutes after that. Derek was heading toward the park. Why would he go there if no one was there?"

"I have no idea," Lexie said, regrouping. "Maybe the boys decided to go there and hang out without me. They did that sometimes because they knew I didn't want to be out too late and worry my parents."

Jared ran his tongue over his teeth. Lexie was a decent liar, and yet he knew she was doing it so it was all for naught. "What did the boys do there when you weren't around?"

"I obviously don't know because I wasn't there," Lexie said. "I … should I have a lawyer?"

"Do you need a lawyer?"

"Um … ."

"Only the guilty need a lawyer, Lexie," Mel said. "If you need one, though, you should tell us now so we can get you one. You're legally an adult, so you have to make the choice on this one."

"I'm not guilty of anything," Lexie argued. "Why would you think I'm guilty of something?"

"We didn't say you were guilty," Jared said. "We're trying to figure out what happened to Derek, and as his girlfriend – and the love of his life – we naturally assumed you knew what was going on with him."

Lexie exhaled heavily, Jared's words causing her to preen. "Derek and I would've been happy forever if this hadn't happened."

"I know," Jared said, his voice grave. "You had your whole future ripped away from you."

"I would think you'd want us to catch whoever killed Derek given that," Mel added.

"I do want you to catch who hurt Derek," Lexie said. "I just can't believe someone would really hurt him. Are you sure he didn't just fall down or something? That's the rumor in town, by the way."

"Well, the medical examiner doesn't seem to believe that," Mel said. "We can't entirely rule it out, though, because it seems Derek was drunk at the time of his death."

Lexie faltered and Jared got the distinct impression that she was surprised – or very good at feigning it – by that little tidbit. "I never saw Derek drink, so I have trouble believing that."

"Science doesn't lie," Jared pointed out. "Are you saying the medical examiner doesn't know what he's doing?"

"Of course not," Lexie scoffed. "It's just … maybe someone slipped something in his Coke. I'll bet that's what happened. Someone slipped something in his Coke when he wasn't looking and he got so drunk he fell down and hit his head."

Jared leaned back in his chair. "Who would do that, Lexie?"

"I … have no idea. Everyone loved Derek."

"If everyone loved Derek, and he never drinks, that means something doesn't add up here," Jared said. "Derek was drunk when he was killed. What do you think that means?"

"I don't know what you want me to say," Lexie said, crossing her arms over her chest. "I wasn't there. I didn't think anyone was there. I don't know why you're treating me like this." His lower lip trembled. "I'm in mourning. Can't you see that?"

Mel and Jared exchanged a look. Lexie Studebaker was quite the actress. She clearly knew more than she was letting on, though.

"Well, I think you should think long and hard about what all of this means," Mel suggested. "This isn't something that's going to go away. My partner and I are going to be working on this until we know exactly what happened to Derek."

"And then someone is going to pay for his murder," Jared added. "I just hope it's the right person, because someone might try to frame someone else in an effort to clear his or herself if we're not careful, and then things are going to get ugly."

"Really ugly," Mel intoned.

"I think I'm done here," Lexie said, her fear and trepidation vanishing in almost an instant. "No, you know what? I'm definitely done here."

SEVENTEEN

"We have to go back out to the Donnelly house," Zander said, causing Harper to shift her eyes from her computer screen. "Why?"

"Because Jenny Porter just ambushed me while I was downtown picking up our lunch – this is why we should never go out on the street when other people are around, by the way – and claims that the house is definitely haunted and we need to do an exorcism right now."

Harper made a face. "We don't do exorcisms."

"That's what I told her and she told me to shut it," Zander said, dropping a deli bag on Harper's desk. "So, as soon as you're done with your lunch, I think you and Eric should go out there."

Harper balked. "Eric and me? No way."

Zander sat at his desk and opened his own bag, fixing Harper with a serious look. "We both know it's time you gave Eric the talk," he said. "If you don't, he's going to spend the next six months moping."

"Why six months?" Harper asked, unwrapping her sandwich. "You don't think Jared is going to bolt after six months, do you?"

Zander made a face. "I think Jared is whipped for life, Harp. Don't flip yourself out over an offhand comment. If you're going to start doing that, I'm going to have to punch you. Since I can't punch a girl, that means I'm really going to have to punch Jared. No one wants that."

"Jared would kick your ass," Harper argued.

"Says you," Zander shot back. "I'm in prime condition, baby. I box at the gym."

"And he's been trained to kill people."

"Yes, but he's all fuzzy-wuzzy over you," Zander said. "He's distracted. I would be on him before he even realized what was happening."

Harper made a mournful face. "I don't want to talk to Eric," she admitted. "Where is he anyway?"

"He's getting lunch down at the hot dog stand on the corner because he's still mad at me," Zander answered.

"He's still mad about yesterday? He needs to get over it."

"That's why you're taking him on this job," Zander said. "He's mad at me because he can't internally rationalize being angry with you. You're his heart's desire. The problem is your heart is already taken, and even if it wasn't he wouldn't be the one you're looking for."

"But . . . ."

"No," Zander said, wagging a finger. "You have to tell him. He's not going to move on unless you make things clear to him. I can't do this for you. He doesn't believe me when I say you're not interested. He doesn't want to believe me."

"I don't want to hurt his feelings."

"I think it's too late for that," Zander said. "That's why you have to do it now."

"Fine."

"Good," Zander said. "Now eat your sandwich and tell me all about your romantic night with Jared. How did sex the second time around go?"

"I hate you sometimes."

"I love you, too."

. . .

"**WHY** ARE WE BACK HERE AGAIN?" Eric grumbled an hour later, trudging up the driveway to the Donnelly house and reminding Harper of a petulant teenager.

"Because Jenny claims more mysterious things have happened and she's going to show us this time," Harper replied. "She's just finishing up a showing at another house and then she's heading in this direction."

"You said there wasn't a ghost here, though. Does she think you're going to magically conjure one?"

"I have no idea," Harper said, studying his dour profile for a moment. "I'm sorry I made you come out here with me. If you want to go back, you can take my car and I'll catch a ride with Jenny."

Eric was instantly contrite. "That's not what I was saying," he said. "I just … I'm sorry."

"You don't have anything to be sorry about," Harper said, sensing her opening. "It's just … ."

Eric cut her off. "Zander sent me out here because he doesn't want to be around me, didn't he?"

"That's not it."

"Are you guys going to fire me because I got in that fight with Zander? If so, I understand. It was completely unprofessional."

Harper sighed. She couldn't put this off another second. "We're not going to fire you, Eric," she said. "You're a great colleague and you have an outstanding work ethic."

"Then why did Zander send me out here with you instead of coming himself?" Eric challenged. "You two are in love with each other again. It's not like he wants to get away from you."

"He sent you with me because he thought we should talk," Harper said, squaring her shoulders. "I think we should talk, too."

"About what?" Eric's face was unreadable.

"You know about what," Harper said, choosing her words carefully. "Here's the thing, Eric … ." She had no idea how to finish the sentence.

"You don't like me *that* way," Eric supplied for her. "I know you don't. I'm sorry if you feel I've been … coming on too strong."

"Personally I'm flattered that you would even think of me in that regard," Harper said. "I really am. I just don't have romantic feelings for you. I hope we can stay friends. I don't want to upset you … or hurt you … or embarrass you. We have to get past this, though."

"You don't like me because of Jared, right?"

"I have very strong feelings for Jared," Harper confirmed. "Even I can't explain how I managed to fall for him so quickly. If Jared didn't exist, though, I still wouldn't have romantic feelings for you. I don't want you getting the wrong idea.

"He's not standing between us," she continued. "He's standing in front of me, which is where I want him to be, but there can never be an us even if Jared disappears tomorrow."

"Well, that was brutally honest," Eric muttered.

"I'm really sorry," Harper offered.

"You don't have to be sorry," Eric said, straightening and extending his hand. "Still friends?"

Harper shook his hand, even though she felt ridiculous doing it, and smiled. "We'll always be friends, Eric."

"Then I have absolutely nothing to complain about."

"**I'M** sorry I'm late. My showing took longer than it was supposed to."

Jenny Porter, her red hair streaming behind her, scampered up the front walk, jangling a set of keys in her hand.

"That's okay," Harper said, pushing herself away from the wall she'd been leaning against. "We haven't been waiting that long."

"It's good to see you, Harper," Jenny said, giving Harper a quick hug and smiling at Eric. "Who are you?"

"I'm sorry," Harper said, remembering her manners. "This is Eric Tyler. He works with Zander and me."

"It's nice to meet you," Jenny said, gracing Eric with what could only be described as a flirtatious smile. "Wait … you only work with Zander, right? You don't do anything else with him, do you?"

Eric forced a tight smile. "We just work together."

"Whew! That's a relief," Jenny said, opening the door of the cottage and fixing Harper with an apologetic look. "I'm wildly attracted to gay guys for some reason. Whenever I look at a guy now and think he's hot I just assume he's gay."

"Welcome to Zander's world," Harper teased.

"Yes, well, I'm afraid I jumped on him downtown," Jenny said, leading Harper and Eric inside. "He didn't look happy to see me."

"That's just his face," Eric said.

Harper ignored the dig. Eric was working overtime to get over his bitterness. She opted to give him a little leeway. "So what happened this time that has you convinced there's a ghost?"

"Everything keeps moving," Jenny explained, stopping in the small living room first. "For example, do you see that lamp by the table over there?"

Harper nodded.

"It's not supposed to be there," she said. "It's supposed to be on that other table and yet it has moved to this one twice. I'm not moving it. No one else is coming in here. If it's not ghosts, how is it moving?"

"Ghosts don't really move lamps," Harper replied.

"Are you saying ghosts don't move things?"

"I ... ." Harper broke off, biting her lip. In truth, ghosts did move things. She'd never heard of them moving a lamp, but stranger things had happened. "What else has moved?"

Jenny moved from the living room into the kitchen and pointed at the counter. "Do you see that canister?"

"The cookie jar?" Harper asked, moving farther into the room.

Jenny nodded. "That cookie jar was on the baker's rack the other day and today it's on the counter," she said.

"Are there cookies in it?" Eric asked.

"What does that matter?"

"I'm just curious if someone moved it to get cookies out," he said. "That might signify that a human was moving things instead of a ghost."

"What human?" Jenny asked, her agitation growing. "I'm the only human coming in here except for the people I show the house to and I can guarantee they're not moving things around. Plus, the cookies in that jar have been there for months. They're stale. No one would eat them."

Harper licked her lips as she scanned the cottage. Nothing seemed out of the ordinary. Nothing felt off. The house was empty. "I don't see a ghost, Jenny," she said, lifting her hands helplessly.

"Do you always see them at all times?" Jenny was starting to get shrill.

"No."

"Well, then it's probably hiding!"

"Hey, kids, what's going on?" Jared appeared in the doorframe, taking everyone by surprise and causing Jenny to clutch at her chest.

"Is he a ghost?"

"He's a police officer," Harper replied dryly, rolling her eyes until they landed on Jared. "You know you can't just walk into a strange house, right? That's technically against the law."

"Not when you leave the keys in the door," Jared said, lifting Jenny's key ring and shaking it. "That's not safe, by the way."

"Oh, thanks," Jenny said, snatching the keys. She took a moment to collect herself and when she did, she turned her full attention to Jared. "You're the new cop, huh?"

Jared nodded. "And you are?"

"Jenny Porter." She extended her hand and shook Jared's, lingering long enough to make Harper feel uncomfortable. "You're not gay, are you?"

Jared made a face. "That's a nice opening line you've got there," he said, pulling his hand back.

"I'm sorry," Jenny said. "Every time I find a man attractive he turns out to be gay."

"That's possibly very flattering," Jared said, turning his attention to Harper. "What are you doing here?"

"This is the real estate agent I told you about," Harper explained. "She thinks there's a ghost here because things keep moving."

"Do you see a ghost?"

Harper shook her head.

"Do you think there's one here?"

"I honestly don't," Harper replied. "I can usually feel a presence long before I see something. I don't feel anything here."

"So, you're not gay?" Jenny asked, her interest in Harper's part of the conversation waning.

"No," Jared answered, winking at Harper.

"Do you want to go to a real estate party with me tonight?" Jenny asked. "I know it's short notice, but you're extremely attractive. I'm taking a shot that you haven't been in town long enough to hook up with anyone."

"You must send off a scent to attract women or something," Eric muttered.

Jared opened his mouth and then snapped it shut, debating how to answer. He took longer than Harper would've liked, though, and she made a disgusted sound in the back of her throat.

"Chill out," Jared ordered. "I was just deciding what I should say."

"Don't let me stand in your way," Harper snapped. "I think you should go to the real estate party."

"I knew this would happen," Eric said.

"Hey, nothing is happening," Jared said, extending a warning finger in Eric's direction. "Don't get any ideas."

"Am I missing something?" Jenny asked.

"No," Harper said.

"Yes," Jared countered. "While I appreciate the offer, I already have a girlfriend."

"You do?" Jenny was disappointed. "Who worked fast enough to nab you? You've only been in town a month."

"Harper nabbed me," Jared answered, smirking at the murderous look on his delightful blonde's face. "She moved in and snapped me up like I was the last stuffed mushroom on the tray."

"That is just … ." Harper shook her head, mortified.

"You're dating him?" Jenny asked, impressed.

"I haven't decided yet," Harper replied, glaring at Jared. "I was this morning. Now he's kind of bugging me."

"She swooped in and stole my heart," Jared said, patting his chest.

"Harper stole my heart." His face was thoughtful. "That's what I'm going to call you."

"What?" Harper was confused.

"Never mind," Jared said, shaking his head. "We'll discuss that later. I only stopped because I saw your car and wanted to see what you were doing. I haven't seen you in four hours and I think I'm going through withdrawal."

"Ugh." Eric rolled his eyes.

"Technically we're not doing anything," Harper said, her cheeks warming at Jared's words. "There's nothing here for me to do."

"You have to do something," Jenny argued. "I can't sell a haunted house."

"Have you considered humans are coming in and moving things?" Jared asked.

Jenny made a "well, duh" face. "No. It never occurred to me."

"I'm just saying that it's unlikely there's a supernatural explanation for this," Jared said. "The most obvious solution is usually the correct one."

"The family lives out of town," Jenny said. "I'm the only one showing the house. No one else is coming in here. I lock the doors whenever I leave."

Jared moved past Jenny and tugged on the sliding glass door behind the kitchen table, pulling it open with minimal effort. "Maybe they're getting in through this unlocked door," he suggested.

"I don't understand," Jenny said. "I checked that when I did my first walkthrough."

Jared hunkered down so he could study the lock. "It looks like someone jimmied it," he said finally. "These doors are easy to open. The lock on this is ancient. You should put a piece of wood in the track here to make sure people can't get it open."

"Okay," Jenny said, flapping her hands. "Now I'm worried that someone is coming in here and doing illegal things, though."

"Like what?" Jared asked.

"I don't know. Maybe they're cooking meth."

"I think you watch too much television," Jared said. "The house would have a noticeable odor if that was going on. Do you have something you can wedge in here?"

Jenny shook her head. "I'll have to come back tomorrow."

"I wouldn't worry about it too much," Jared offered, tugging the door shut again. "It's probably kids looking to hang out without parental eyes prying into their business. It doesn't look like they're doing too much damage."

"Well, at least it's not a ghost," Jenny said, her pragmatic side taking over.

"That's something to be happy about," Harper said.

Jenny sighed. "Well, that's one problem solved," she said, turning her predatory gaze to Eric. "I just have one other problem to deal with today. I don't suppose you want to go to a real estate dinner with me, do you?"

Eric groaned. "I just watched you ask Jared out."

"He's got a girlfriend." Jenny wasn't bothered by Eric's attitude. "I'll bet you look good in a suit."

"I'm out of here," Eric muttered, breezing past Harper. "This day just ... sucks."

"Welcome to my world," Jenny sighed.

EIGHTEEN

"Well that was fun," Jared said, walking down the cottage's driveway and waving as Jenny sped off. "She's ... neat."

"She's not so bad," Harper said, her eyes landing on Eric as he paced behind her car. She couldn't be sure, but it looked like he was talking to himself.

"What's his deal?"

"We had a talk before Jenny showed up and he's ... unhappy with his lot in life," Harper replied.

"What did you talk about?"

Harper met Jared's twinkling gaze and made a face. "You think you're something special, don't you?"

"I think *you're* something special," Jared replied, grabbing her hand and squeezing it. "That's why I stopped to get my Harper fix when I should be working."

"I can't even pretend to be angry with you when you say sweet things like that," Harper said. "You're just too ... cute."

"Luckily for you I'm cute and not gay," Jared said, leaning over and giving her a quick kiss. "I'm going to do that better later. I don't want to risk enraging Eric."

"He's not really angry," Harper explained. "He's … hurt more than anything else."

"I think he's disappointed," Jared corrected. "Who wouldn't be? He lost the best girl in the world … to me."

Harper grabbed his face with both of her hands. "I can't help wanting to kiss you senseless when you say things like that."

"Don't fight it."

Harper gave him a firm kiss. "Better?"

"For now," Jared said, taking a step back. "What are you going to do now?"

"I'm not sure," Harper replied. "I was thinking of letting Eric take my car back and walking through the woods." She pointed toward the tree line at the back of the cottage.

"Why?"

"Don't you know where that leads?"

Jared shook his head. "I guess I'm still figuring out the geography here," he said, glancing around. "What's on the other side of those trees?"

"Well, it's about a mile walk, but it leads to the town park," Harper said. "This river is the one I was telling you about the other night. Some of the kids party alongside it."

"Are you hoping to see Derek?"

"That would be nice," Harper conceded. "I'm not betting on that, though. I just want to look around. I still think those kids were doing something in the woods that night. Maybe I'll get lucky and find whatever it is they're trying to hide."

"I think that's a fabulous idea," Jared said. "I'm going to go with you."

Harper's eyebrows flew up her forehead. "You are?"

"I am," Jared said. "I've been considering going through the woods behind where Derek died myself. I might as well go with someone who knows where she's going so I don't get lost. You would cry if I never left those woods."

"Do you want me to invite Eric?"

"What do you think?"

Harper smirked. "I'll send him back to the office," she said. "You're going to have to leave your car here and then circle back around for it."

"Oh, no," Jared said. "We're going to walk back to your office and get your car together and then you're going to drive me back here to get my car when we're done. That ensures at least a full hour with you. I'm going to treat it like my afternoon snack."

"You're lucky you're smoking hot," Harper chided, moving toward her car. "Another woman might think that's a cheesy line."

"That's why I picked you."

"I thought I swooped in and snapped you up?" Harper challenged.

"I didn't say I wasn't thrilled with the swooping."

"SO, wait ... tell me exactly what I'm looking at geographically here," Jared instructed twenty minutes later, his fingers linked with Harper's as she led him closer to the riverbank. "This river winds a lot. This is the same river that pops up over by your house, right?"

"Yes," Harper replied. "It's not even remotely straight. It cuts through quite a few different pockets around here. In fact, because the trees are so dense in some spots, it's virtually impossible to walk the bank throughout the entire town if you want to do it."

Jared rolled his neck until it cracked. "That means that some of the areas are isolated," he surmised. "That makes it easier for people to party."

"You think like a cop," Harper said. "It also makes it easier for people to fish and have private picnics."

Jared smirked. "Would you like to have a private picnic with me by the river one day?"

"Are you going to cook?"

"I think I can be persuaded to cook if you promise that we'll be alone for the entire afternoon."

"Deal," Harper said, rolling up to the balls of her feet and planting a soft kiss on his cheek. "We have a spot behind our house where we hung a hammock by the river. It's beautiful, and no one ever comes by."

"You have a hammock?" Jared was intrigued. "I've always wanted to take a nap in a hammock. I have no idea why. I think I saw it in a movie once."

"We can definitely take a nap in the hammock," Harper said, turning her attention back to the riverbank. "When we were teenagers, this is generally where we came to party."

"No offense, but you don't strike me as the partying type."

"I really wasn't," Harper admitted. "Wait … was that an insult?"

"It was a compliment," Jared replied. "I wasn't a big partier myself. I'm taking it Zander was a partier."

Harper shrugged. "Zander was … a social butterfly," she said. "He still is. I like time alone, but Zander never really has enjoyed hanging out by himself. He makes me go with him to get a pedicure because he can't take it if it's too quiet."

"That can remain a thing you two do alone."

Harper giggled. "He liked to come to a few parties down here back in the day, and I had to come with him because I was always worried someone would pick on him."

"Mel says that Zander worried people would pick on you, too," Jared said. "How rough was it when you started doing miraculous things and people figured out you were talking to ghosts?"

"Um … ." Harper didn't know how to answer the question. She instinctively moved to pull her hand away from Jared, but he stopped her.

"No," he said. "Tell me."

"It wasn't easy," Harper said, running her free hand through her hair. "I told myself it didn't matter what they thought, but sometimes it hurt. I'm not going to lie. It doesn't bother me now. Somewhere along the way I figured out that I wanted to be me and I was fine if other people didn't like or accept me. I wish I would've figured it out in high school because it would've made my life easier."

Jared tugged her to him, wrapping her in a warm hug and kissing her ear. "I like and accept you for exactly who you are," he whispered. "You're perfect just the way you are, Heart."

Harper stilled. "Heart?"

"That's what I'm going to call you," Jared said, rocking her slightly. "It's close to your name and every time I see you my heart jumps."

Despite herself, Harper couldn't help but feel a warm glow build throughout her chest. "I think I might cry."

"Don't you dare," Jared ordered, pulling his head back so he could study her face. "It's not supposed to be a sad thing. You're supposed to think I'm charming and smother me with kisses."

"Well, in that case ... ." Harper slammed her mouth into Jared's, taking him by surprise with the force of the kiss. He enthusiastically returned it, splaying his hands over her back and pressing her as close to him as he could manage.

When they finally separated, Jared was breathless. "That was ... ."

"Pretty good," Harper finished. "I'll do better when we're in the hammock."

"I'm definitely looking forward to that," Jared said, grabbing her hand and urging her back into the woods. "Come on. I want to finish our hike so I can go back to work. The faster I get through this day, the faster we can do that again."

"You make laugh."

"You make me smile," Jared countered.

By the time the couple made it to the park they were mired in a mutual adoration society that neither one of them could explain. Silently they decided to embrace it, because explaining it seemed impossible.

"And we're back to where this all started," Jared said, his eyes landing on the merry-go-round. "I didn't see anything that would lead me to believe anything heavy has been happening in these woods. Did you?"

Harper shook her head. "That doesn't mean nothing is out there," she cautioned. "We walked one path. There are quite a few more of them out there. I'm not sure you could find anything if you didn't know exactly where to look."

"What are you doing back here?" Derek asked, popping into view and causing Harper to rear back and smack into Jared's chest.

"What's wrong?" Jared asked, looking around as he steadied her.

"It's Derek," Harper gritted out, catching her breath. "He just ... surprised me."

"Obviously," Jared said dryly, glaring at the empty spot in front of Harper. "Have some manners, dude. Don't scare someone just because you can."

"He can't see me, can he?" Derek asked, waving his hand in front of Jared's face.

"No, he can't," Harper said, smoothing her shirt. "Stop doing that."

"What is he doing?" Jared asked.

"Being a pain."

"I'm not a pain," Derek argued. "I'm just ... being a ghost. Isn't that what ghosts do?"

"I think it depends on what kind of ghost you want to be," Harper replied. "What kind of ghost do you want to be?"

"The kind who scares the crap out of assholes," Derek replied, not missing a beat.

"I'm the only one who can see you," Harper pointed. "You can't ... wait a second. Are you insinuating I'm an asshole?"

Jared chuckled. "Those are fighting words. Of course, I can't see you to fight, so that makes things a little more difficult."

"You're not an asshole," Derek said. "That's not what I meant. You're really not so bad."

"Thanks for the compliment."

"If he's hitting on you ... smack him or something," Jared instructed.

"He's not very smart, is he?" Derek asked.

"He's very smart," Harper said. "He's just ... out of his element."

"I heard that," Jared muttered.

Harper sucked in a steadying breath and tried to focus the conversation on something helpful. "Have you remembered anything?"

"I keep running into a dark wall," Derek said. "I remember leaving my house after I got the call from David ... and then nothing."

"Did you talk to David today?" Harper asked Jared. "I forgot to ask."

"We talked to Lexie, Dylan, and Brandon," Jared replied. "David is still technically a minor and his parents refused to bring him into the station."

"That's interesting," Harper mused. "He's the one who called Derek and he's conveniently the only one you can't talk to. What did the other kids say?"

"They all lied and said they weren't at the park and had no idea why Derek was there."

"Do you remember seeing any of them?" Harper asked Derek. "Think hard."

"What do you think I've been doing for the past three days?" Derek grumbled. "I just told you that I keep running into a wall when it comes to that night. I don't know how to remember."

"I'm not accusing you of anything," Harper said, her voice calm as her temper flared. "We're having trouble figuring out what happened to you. We know it was something bad. All your friends are lying for a reason. You must have some ... inkling ... why that is."

"You don't seem to understand what I'm saying," Derek snapped. "There's nothing in my head."

Harper swallowed the mad urge to laugh as she tried to ignore his unintended insult against himself. "Okay, let's try this from a different angle," she suggested. "Were you and your friends doing anything you weren't supposed to be doing?"

Derek furrowed his brow. "Why would you think that?"

"That wasn't an answer," Harper pressed. "We know you guys were doing ... something ... out here that you didn't want anyone to know about. What was it?"

"We weren't doing anything but hanging out."

He was lying. Harper didn't know how she knew that, but it was obvious. "We can't help you if you don't help us."

"You can't help me no matter what," Derek seethed. "I'm already dead!"

"There's no reason to yell at me," Harper shot back. "I can help you move over to the other side when you're ready. There's something … better … out there for you. You're obviously not ready yet, though. You want someone to pay for what happened to you and we can't make that happen until we know how you died.

"I think you're putting this wall up because part of you doesn't want to remember what happened that night," she continued. "You're the one making this more difficult than it has to be."

"You're talking to me as if I care about helping you," Derek said. "I don't care about helping you."

"Then maybe you should care about helping yourself," Harper suggested. "Or, better yet, why don't you consider helping your parents. Do you think that struggling through your death and wondering how you died at the same time is good for them? They want answers."

"I can't give them any answers," Derek exploded. "I can't do anything but watch my mother cry and my father drink. I've spent hours trying to reach out to them. They can't see me. They can't hear me."

"They can still love you," Harper interjected. "They're your parents. They weren't meant to outlive you. If they're going to have a chance to move past this then they're going to need closure. You're the only one who can give them that."

"And what if I never remember?"

"Then someone is going to get away with murder," Harper replied, unruffled. "You have to decide what's more important. If it's protecting so-called friends who are running around and pretending to be sorry about your death instead of legitimately mourning you, then I guess that's on you.

"Whatever you decide, you know where I live and where to find me," she continued. "Until then, I don't know how to help you. We're stuck. I won't come back here again. If you want help, you're going to have to come to me. I'm done bending over backward to help someone who obviously doesn't want to be helped."

Derek was flabbergasted. He watched Harper walk away, Jared at her side, and felt helpless. He had no idea what to do.

"That was pretty terrifying, Heart," Jared said, squeezing Harper's hand as they trudged away. "If I wasn't already impressed with you, that would've sealed the deal."

"He needs a kick in the pants," Harper said. "You can't be petulant, pouty, and annoying and expect answers to miraculously appear. He needs to be proactive if we're going to get anywhere."

"You amaze me."

Harper mustered a genuine smile. "Just wait until I get you in that hammock."

"Be still my heart."

NINETEEN

"What are you doing today?" Jared asked the next morning, drying his hair with a towel as he watched Harper shimmy into a pair of blue jeans. For a moment, he considered trying to get her back out of the jeans, but he knew he would be late for work if he tried and Mel wouldn't find his libido an acceptable excuse for missing work.

"Well, I had an idea," Harper admitted, absentmindedly running her hand over Jared's flat stomach. "How often do you work out?"

"As often as I can," Jared replied, chuckling. "If you keep doing that I'm going to be late for work and you're going to have to explain to Mel why because he'll throttle me if I do it."

Harper giggled. "Sorry. Your stomach is like a work of art, though. It boggles my mind someone could be this perfect."

"That's what I think every time I look at you," Jared said, dropping a quick kiss on her mouth before taking a step back. "You're going to distract me if you don't keep your distance."

"Okay," Harper said, gracing him with a rueful smile. "I can't wait until this case is solved and we can spend a day together without having to go to work."

"I'm right there with you," Jared said. "Tell me about your idea."

"You just said I couldn't distract you."

Jared smirked. "Not *that* idea, trouble. Tell me about the other idea you had regarding work."

"Oh, that," Harper said, making a face. "I think I might have worked something out in my head while I was sleeping last night. I didn't wake up again, by the way. You're definitely magic."

"Or I'm just giving you a workout and you're too exhausted to wake up," Jared countered. "Either way I look like a hero … carry on."

"Someone has been breaking into the old Donnelly house," Harper said.

"So?"

"It's only ten minutes from the park if you're walking in a straight line," Harper said. "What if you were right and kids – our kids – are the ones breaking into the house?"

Jared stilled. "That's an interesting theory," he said. "To what end? They're not cooking meth in there no matter what your friend Jenny thinks."

"No, but they could be drinking and partying in there," Harper said. "They could be doing other stuff. We have no idea who is breaking into the house. Very few people would do it, though. The cottage is in close proximity to the park. I think it's worth checking out."

"What are you going to check out?" Jared asked, confused.

"The house."

"I don't understand," Jared admitted. "If the house is being broken into, it's happening when it's dark out. What do you think you're going to find during the day?"

"We don't know that the house is being broken into at night," Harper countered. "We know the house is being broken into when Jenny isn't there. There's a difference."

"And I'm still not getting it."

"Jenny works for Martin Real Estate," Harper supplied.

"Good for her."

"You're starting to bug me," Harper gritted out. "Tim Martin owns Martin Real Estate. His oldest son is David Martin."

"Oh," Jared said, realization dawning. "You think that David could know when the house is being shown and using it when it's empty. You're a smart cookie."

"Thank you."

"I have a question, though," Jared said. "If David has access to his father's office, why wouldn't he just steal the key to get into the house? Why go in through the back?"

"His father would notice if he stole the key and kept it," Harper replied. "Maybe he stole it once and left the back door open. You said it looked jimmied, but it's old. That might be normal wear and tear."

"I like this idea except for one thing," Jared said.

"What's that?"

"If you're right, I don't want you going to that house alone," Jared replied. "Those kids outnumber you and we have no idea what they're capable of. They might've killed Derek."

"I'm just going to spy and see if I can catch a glimpse of them going inside."

"Not alone you're not," Jared argued. "I can't go with you because Mel secured an interview with David and his parents. I know he won't be at that house today. I still don't want you going alone."

"I'll take Zander with me."

"And Eric."

Now it was Harper's turn to be surprised. "You want me to take Eric with me? Since when?"

"Since I want you having as much backup as humanly possible," Jared answered. "I'm pretty fond of you, Harper Harlow. I don't want you in danger. You either agree to take Zander and Eric with you or I'm handcuffing you to the bed."

"That would sound kinky under different circumstances."

"That's the deal," Jared said. "If you go there alone we're going to have our first big fight ... and, Heart, it's going to be a doozy."

"I STILL DON'T UNDERSTAND why we all have to do this," Eric complained an hour later, shoving Zander to the side so he could get comfortable on the hard ground beneath the large willow tree on the east side of the Donnelly house. "Isn't this a one-person job? Two at the most?"

Harper sighed. "I promised Jared we would all come together. If you don't like it, call him and complain. I'm sure he would love to hear from you."

"Maybe I will."

"I think it's fun," Molly enthused, crossing her legs over one another and reaching into her box of Milk Duds. "It's like we're at a movie."

"Yeah, one of those really boring art house ones that no one cares about," Zander said, resting his back against the tree. "I think it's cute that Jared wants to protect you, Harp, but this is a little ridiculous."

"What's ridiculous about it?"

"There are four of us sitting under a tree hoping that one big bush is going to hide us," Zander replied. "We're waiting for possibly murderous teenagers to break into a house that until yesterday was thought to be haunted."

"You're giving me a headache," Harper grumbled, rubbing her forehead. "Don't you think it's too much of a coincidence that Martin Real Estate is handling the sale of this cottage and that it's only ten minutes away from where Derek was killed?"

"Not really."

"I agree with Zander," Eric said. "If this was such a great lead I think Jared would be out here doing surveillance himself."

"I'm surprised he didn't want to do surveillance with Harper so they could make out all afternoon," Molly said. "That's sounds like a better way to do something like this."

"That *does* sound like a better way," Harper agreed. "He's meeting with the Martins. David is still technically a minor, so his parents managed to keep Mel and Jared from questioning him yesterday. They worked out some arrangement to do it today."

"Do you really think Derek was murdered by his own friends?" Molly asked. "If you ask me, that's the worst way to go."

Harper cast her a sidelong look, searching for hints Molly was worried or uneasy. On the contrary, she looked happier than she had in weeks. Harper realized Eric was right when he said Molly just wanted to be part of the group. She was the only one not complaining about their current predicament.

"It does sound like the worst way to go," Harper said. "I don't know if his friends killed him. I do think those kids know something that they're keeping to themselves. I have no idea why. You would think they'd want to help the police."

"Not if they're guilty," Zander countered. "All they care about is covering their own butts. They weren't really friends with Derek so his death is nothing more than a minor inconvenience. There's a reason that most teenagers profile as sociopaths."

"Did you see that on *Dateline*?"

Zander grinned. "I like true crime. Sue me."

"It's sad to think Derek didn't have any true friends," Harper lamented. "High school sucks when you have people to love. I had my best friend in the world and I would've been crushed if something happened to him. None of these kids really seem to care that Derek is dead."

"Oh, I would've been crushed if something happened to me, too," Zander teased, pressing a quick kiss to Harper's cheek. "I would've killed myself if something happened to you."

"I know," Harper said, patting his knee. "I ... ." She broke off when a hint of furtive movement at the corner of the cottage caught her attention.

"What were you going to say?" Molly asked.

Harper lifted a finger to her lips to silence everyone and then pointed toward a shadowy figure as it moved toward the sliding glass door. Everyone peered in the direction Harper indicated, the only sound ragged breathing as they watched a hoodie-clad figure play around with the lock and open the door. The person disappeared inside after a moment, dragging the door shut and leaving them able to talk again.

"What do you think?" Molly whispered.

"I think there's only one of them and I'm dying to see who it is,"

Harper said, getting to her feet. "We need to split up. Eric and Molly, you go by the front door in case he tries to escape. Zander and I are going to go in through the back."

"We are?" Zander whined. "Shouldn't we call Jared instead?"

"I don't want to wait. I have to know."

"Fine," Zander grumbled, pushing himself to a standing position. "If this goes badly, though, I'm going to smack you around."

"Duly noted."

The group split up, Eric and Molly creeping toward the front of the house as Zander and Harper hurried toward the back door. They didn't want to give the individual time to hide. Harper glanced inside the kitchen, immediately finding what she was looking for when the figure opened the refrigerator and looked inside. He – and Harper was sure it was a man given his broad shoulders – appeared unaware that he was being watched.

Harper pushed the sliding glass door open, cringing at the noise, and walked inside. Zander followed, his heart pounding as he took a protective position at Harper's side. The person at the refrigerator apparently didn't hear the noise.

Zander cleared his throat. "Who goes there?"

Harper made a face at the odd greeting, and when the individual swiveled she expected to find a familiar face. Instead, the one that greeted her had more lines than any teenager would ever boast and a terrified expression on his grizzled face.

"I'm sorry," the man said, instantly contrite. "I didn't mean to break in. I was just … hungry."

Harper took a moment to look over the stranger, her heart rolling when she realized what she was seeing. She should've noticed the aged denim and mismatched boots from outside. This wasn't some hardened criminal. It was a homeless and starving man looking to survive.

"It's okay," Harper said, sympathy washing over her. "We won't hurt you."

"No," Zander agreed. "In fact … how does pizza sound? I'll order a few and we'll have a party."

If Harper ever needed to be reminded why Zander was her best friend, she knew she would pick this moment in time to reflect upon. Zander saw what she did and immediately decided to help. That's what made him a great man ... and the only friend she would ever truly need.

"That sounds great," Harper said, smiling. "We'll get pizza for everyone and talk. How does that sound?"

The man opened his mouth and closed it, stunned and overwhelmed. "Aren't you going to call the police?"

"No way," Zander replied. "They'll eat all of our pizza. We can't have that."

"What's your name?" Harper asked.

"Jeff Clarke."

"Well, Jeff Clarke, it's nice to meet you. I'm Harper Harlow and this is Zander Pritchett. We have two other friends here, but they're nice, too. Let's order some pizza."

TWENTY

"Not that I'm not happy to see you – and I'm always happy to see you – but what's the big emergency?" Jared asked three hours later, hopping out of his truck and striding toward Harper as she paced the Donnelly driveway.

"I ... ." Harper's face was flushed, her hands jittery, and the look she sent Jared was one of pure worry.

"What's wrong?" Jared asked, softening his voice and taking a step toward her. He put his hands on her shoulders, rubbing them softly before moving to cup her chin. "Tell me."

"I think you're about to be really angry with me," Harper admitted.

"Okay."

"I think you're probably going to yell and swear."

"Okay," Jared said, mentally preparing himself for doomsday. "I'm ready to hear it."

"I ... ." Harper couldn't get the words out. Even though she knew it probably wouldn't happen, real fear regarding Jared's imminent reaction coursed through her. "If you're going to leave after ... ."

"Stop right there," Jared ordered. "You've worked yourself into a frenzy over what I'm assuming is going to turn out to be nothing. I'm not going anywhere. Even if you did something stupid, that doesn't mean I'm somehow going to stop caring about you.

"This is new for both of us," he continued. "I can't fix this until you tell me what happened."

"Well, I brought everyone with me for the stakeout like you asked," Harper said, wetting her lips. "We sat under the willow tree over there and talked for a little bit … Molly brought Milk Duds."

Jared tamped down the inclination to laugh. "Okay."

"We saw someone go in through the sliding glass door," Harper admitted, ripping the Band-Aid off.

"Who? Was it one of the kids?" Jared was curious. "We pulled David Martin in, but his father refused to let him answer any questions so we just sat there staring at each other for fifteen minutes before cutting him loose. It was a total waste of time. We're back to being at a dead end. If you saw one of the other kids enter this place it would be helpful, especially since you have witnesses and we don't have to take the word of a ghost."

Harper shook her head. "We couldn't see who it was from where we were," she said. "He was wearing a hoodie."

"That's okay," Jared said. "Did you think I would be angry at you because you couldn't see who was going into the house? Harper, that's ridiculous."

"I'm not done yet," Harper said, causing Jared's heart to plummet.

"We're about to get to the part I won't like, aren't we?"

Harper nodded. "I had to see who it was," she explained. "We split up. Eric took Molly around to the front and Zander and I followed the person into the house through the sliding glass door. We confronted him in the kitchen."

"Well, I'm already not liking it," Jared said, although he didn't drop his hands from Harper's face. "Tell me the rest of it."

"It wasn't one of the kids," Harper said. "It was a homeless man. His name is Jeff Clarke and he's been breaking into the house to shower and eating stale cookies to survive."

Jared's heart rolled. "Did he touch you?"

"No," Harper said, frustrated. "He's very nice. He's just down on his luck."

"Well, while I'm unhappy with what you did because you could've gotten hurt, you had backup and are standing in front of me," Jared said. "I think we'll survive with only a minor fight tonight. Does that make you feel better?"

"I'm not done," Harper said.

Jared sighed. "Lay it on me."

"He was afraid of us ... and he's really torn up from sleeping outside and being transient for six months ... so we ordered pizza and had a little party and talked to him inside," Harper explained. "So we technically trespassed and threw a party."

Jared pursed his lips. "I see. Is that all?"

Harper shook her head again.

"You need to get it all out there, honey," Jared said. "I'm starting to lose my patience."

"He told us he's been hanging around the woods for weeks and he saw all the kids the night Derek died," Harper said. "They didn't see him because he was hiding. He saw all the teens we've been looking at – including Lexie – and there was a big argument going on. He couldn't hear what it was about. We showed him photos we managed to scrounge up on our cell phones by getting people to text us. He identified everyone who was at the school that day, plus Derek."

"That doesn't surprise me," Jared said. "We knew they were involved. He didn't see Derek die, did he?"

"No."

"Is that all?"

"One more thing," Harper said. "I want to help him and I'm begging you not to arrest him for breaking and entering. If you try, I'm going to claim I was the one who was doing it and you're going to have to arrest me instead and my mother is going to hate you forever."

Jared made an exasperated sound in the back of his throat. "Is that all?"

Harper bit her lip and nodded, letting out a relieved gasp when Jared pulled her in for a hug. "I'm not angry with you," he murmured, rubbing the back of her head. "I'm not thrilled with you, but I'm not angry with you. You have a huge heart. You did a good thing here today. I don't see any reason we have to tell Jenny what you found. We'll clean up the house and find a place for this man. What did you say his name was again?"

"Jeff Clarke," Harper replied. "He's fifty and he's a veteran. He lost his house in Detroit because he has PTSD and he can't be around loud noises."

Jared's heart went out to the man and he hadn't even met him yet. "We're going to fix this," he said, kissing Harper's cheek. "You need to have a little faith in me. I would never arrest a man for trying to survive. I would never be angry with you for trying to help him."

Hope flitted across Harper's face, the naked raw emotion almost causing Jared's knees to buckle. "Even if I broke the law while doing it?"

"You didn't break the law," Jared argued.

Harper arched a challenging eyebrow.

"Okay, you technically broke the law," he conceded. "It was just a little misdemeanor, though. Thankfully you're sleeping with a cop. I can fix all of this."

"Thank you." Harper threw her arms around his neck and Jared hugged her again, internally laughing at the drama.

"Does Zander think I'm going to arrest him, too?" Jared asked, glancing at the house.

"He's hiding in the closet," Harper replied. "He swore he'd never go back in the closet after middle school and now I can't get him out."

"We'll fix this," Jared said. "Come on. I want to meet Jeff and get his statement, and then we'll find a place for him to stay. I promise this is going to be okay."

"COME IN," Jared said, opening the door to his rental house and allowing Harper entrance later that evening. He was dressed down in simple jeans and a T-shirt, and yet Harper didn't think he'd ever looked more appealing.

After introducing Jared to Jeff, the engaging police officer immediately put Jeff at ease as he ate pizza and questioned him about what he saw the night Derek died. Zander eventually came out of the closet and pretended nothing happened, and once he was finished Jared drove Jeff to his house and set him up in the apartment over the garage.

Harper was amazed by his giving spirit, and she greeted Jared with a rambunctious hug the second the door closed.

"This is a nice greeting," Jared laughed, lifting her feet off the ground as he returned the hug. "Did you miss me that much?"

"You've been great today."

"Only today?" Jared challenged. "I think I've been great since you met me."

"Other than that whole trying to arrest me and then leaving town and not calling for ten days thing, right?" Harper asked, refusing to let Jared's ego get too big.

Jared slipped his fingers inside Harper's belt loops and tugged her hips so they were flush with his. "You're supposed to let me off the hook for that stuff."

"I have," Harper said. "I just like keeping you on your toes."

"You've definitely done that," Jared said, dropping a soft kiss on her lips and then pulling away when he heard the back door of the house open. "No offense, but I don't want to maul you in front of Jeff. He's a little jumpy."

"I understand," Harper said. "We'll be able to maul each other in your bedroom after he goes to sleep."

"You're staying here with me tonight?" Jared asked, pleased and surprised at the same time. "What about Zander?"

"He was so worked up about having to hide in the closet today he went out and picked up a guy to find something wrong with," Harper replied. "He'll be okay."

"I like this," Jared said, lifting his chin and smiling as Jeff walked into the living room. "I thought we would order Chinese. Do you like Chinese, Jeff?"

Jeff's expression brightened when he saw Harper. "I'll eat anything. Literally."

An invisible hand squeezed Jared's heart, but he shrugged it away. "What do you want? I figured we'd order quite a few things so we have leftovers for the next few days. I picked up a menu the other day … here it is." Jared scooped it off the coffee table and handed it to Jeff. "Tell me what you like."

Jeff was embarrassed. "I'll eat anything."

Sympathy washed over Harper and she took the menu from him. "I'll pick. I like being in charge."

"I can vouch for that," Jared said, smiling fondly at her. "Sit down, Jeff. I have a few things to catch you up on. You were out in the apartment longer than I expected."

"I didn't want to bother you," Jeff admitted. "I … ."

"You're not a bother," Jared said, cutting him off. "In fact, I'm going to be glad to have you around. This place is a rental, but I can't keep up with everything, so I thought you might like to work around here for the next few days to help me out. That will allow you to earn some money while we move forward."

Harper's heart swelled as Jeff swallowed hard.

"I could do that," Jeff said.

"And when you're caught up here, we need help at our house, too," Harper said, earning a smile from Jared. "Zander is a wonder in the kitchen, but he refuses to do manual labor because he only likes to sweat at the gym."

"I really appreciate everything you guys are doing, but I feel guilty that you're going out of your way for me after I broke the law," Jeff said.

"Don't bring that up again," Jared chided. "You didn't do anything horrible – other than convincing the real estate agent that the cottage was haunted – and you helped in my investigation. On that front, I called Mel and told him what we have and we're pulling every one of those kids back in tomorrow. They're not leaving without giving us some answers."

"That's a relief," Harper said.

"What about you two?" Jeff asked.

"What about us?" Jared was confused. "We're happy as clams. Wait … are clams really happy?"

"I have no idea," Harper said. "I know we're going to be happy with a few shrimp entrees in a few minutes, though. Do you like shrimp, Jeff? Or would you rather have chicken or beef? Or, heck, are you a vegetarian? There's plenty of stuff on the menu without meat if you don't want it."

"You can't be a vegetarian on the street," Jeff said. "I … what about you two needing time alone? I don't want to get in your way. You've been too kind as it is."

"We haven't done anything yet," Jared argued. "Stop talking nonsense and help Harper pick out food. Make sure you order those crab puff things. I love those."

"I just don't feel right about this," Jeff said.

"Jeff, you're tying yourself into knots over nothing," Harper said. "Jared probably won't even be here most of the time. He'll spend a lot of his nights at my house."

Jared smirked. "You're awfully sure about yourself," he teased. "I find that funny given how you thought I was going to have a melt-down this afternoon."

"Yes, well, I've had time to think that over and I realize I might have been a little dramatic," Harper said.

"Might?"

"Fine. I was overly dramatic," Harper conceded. "Zander worked me into a frenzy, though. You know how he is."

"I like him," Jeff said, chuckling. "He kept going on and on about my great shabby chic wardrobe."

"He's funny," Jared agreed. "Harper is right, though. I will be spending a lot of nights at her place. Even when I'm here, though, you're not a bother. You have your own apartment over the garage. We're going to make this work until we figure out a permanent solution. I don't want to hear another argument. Are we clear?"

Jeff mock saluted. "Yes, sir."

"Now, let's get to ordering," Jared said. "I'm starving."

TWENTY-ONE

"Every single one of them has a lawyer," Mel said the next morning, crossing his arms over his chest and eyeing the four teenagers in the conference room. "That's mighty telling."

"They know they're in trouble," Jared said. "The only one who doesn't look worried is Tim Martin. He either believes his kid or knows something we don't."

"He believes his kid," Mel said dryly. "Trust me. That guy is one of those people who thinks his son can never do anything wrong. Whatever David does is justified ... even if he's the one in the wrong."

"How do you know that?"

"Because he stood with his cousin Jim Stone during the whole Zander fiasco ten years ago," Mel replied. "He's a snake."

Jared stilled. "I'm confused. How did he stand with Jim Stone? What did he have to do with all of that?"

"He was on the school board," Mel explained.

"We need to have a talk about that situation one day," Jared said. "We don't have time now, but I want more details. Zander seemed pained to tell the story and Harper started swearing like a sailor when I brought it up."

"Harper is feisty when she wants to be," Mel said, chuckling.

"Yeah, well, I don't like what happened to them and I'm not sure I understand everything," Jared said. "I don't understand how something like that could happen."

"Whisper Cove is tiny and this was ten years ago," Mel said. "Things change."

"Not that much," Jared said. "We don't have time for it now either. Are you ready for this?"

"How do you want to approach them?" Mel asked, his jaw clenching as his mind returned to the task at hand.

"Hard," Jared replied, pushing open the door and entering the room.

"I want to know what you think you're going to accomplish here," Tim Martin announced before Jared and Mel could sit. "I told you yesterday that my son isn't going to answer any of your questions. I see you're bucking for a lawsuit by bringing him in two days in a row. If that's what you want, well … I guess that's what you're going to get."

"Sit down, Tim," Mel ordered, unruffled. "If you want to play the lawsuit game we can do that later. Right now we're dealing with murder. We have priorities in this department."

"Since when?" Tim shot back.

"Sit down, Mr. Martin," Jared ordered, his tone chilly.

Tim was taken aback. "Excuse me? You can't talk to me that way."

"I just did," Jared said.

"We don't have to stand for this," Tim argued, puffing out his chest. "These kids are not under arrest."

"If you would prefer, we can put them under arrest," Mel offered.

"On what grounds?" one of the lawyers asked, exchanging a look with another stuffed suit standing behind Lexie.

"We know they've been lying about being with Derek the night he died," Jared replied, opening a file as he sat down across from them. "By the end of this interview, they're either going to tell the truth or be taken into custody. It's entirely up to them."

"How … I don't understand," Tim said, adjusting his tone. "How can you know they were lying?"

"It's interesting that you don't immediately jump to the conclusion that they're telling the truth and our information is wrong," Mel mused, sitting next to Jared. "That tells me you've already figured out they're lying, too."

"I've done nothing of the sort," Tim argued. "I believe in my son's innocence."

"Well, you won't for long," Jared said. "Okay, since Mr. Martin likes to hear himself talk, we're going to start with David's part in all of this first. Don't worry, you other three will get you turn. So, David, is there anything you want to tell us?"

David, all bravado lost, shrank in his chair. "I didn't do anything."

"See! You heard him," Tim blustered.

"Either shut up or get out, Mr. Martin," Jared instructed. "I'm done playing games with these kids. I've had it with all of them."

Tim snapped his mouth shut.

"That's what I thought," Jared said. "David, we know that you called Derek at around nine the night he died. We got a tip that you did, and we had Verizon pull your phone records and it's been confirmed.

"Before you deny anything, you should also know that we're aware you guys were partying out there on a regular basis and Derek was under the assumption that you would be partying out there again that night," he continued. "We know that Derek arrived, and we have a witness who places all four of you in the woods with Derek that night. You were heard arguing by said witness, and you're believed to be the last four to see Derek alive."

"Who is this witness?" one of the lawyers asked.

"We're not at liberty to discuss that right now," Jared replied. "Suffice it to say that he identified all four suspects and the deceased. He put the time at shortly before eleven. The medical examiner puts Derek's death at shortly after midnight. Can you explain that?"

"I wasn't there," Lexie said.

"Don't lie," Jared said, wagging a finger for emphasis. "You've done nothing but lie since I met you and I've had it."

"You can't talk to me that way," Lexie hissed. "I'm not even supposed to be here. I'm supposed to be at Derek's family's special ceremony at the cemetery. You guys set this up for this exact time so I would miss it."

"I'm sorry you're going to miss out on your little show, but those are the breaks," Jared said. "You got to preen for everyone at the funeral yesterday so you shouldn't miss the graveside service today. You'll have to find another venue to be the center of attention at from here on out. In fact, I think they're going to love you in prison."

Lexie's face drained of color. "Prison? You can't be serious."

"Oh, I'm serious," Jared said. "Right now we have enough evidence to arrest you."

"It's all circumstantial," Brandon's attorney argued.

"That doesn't change the fact that the county prosecutor has agreed to issue warrants," Jared replied. "They're in the other room."

"That means everyone in town will hear about this," Tim spat. "You can't do that. It will ruin my business."

"Yes, because that's what's important here," Mel deadpanned, rolling his eyes. "Forget the dead boy. Let's worry about your real estate business."

"Don't push me, Mel. I'll have your job!"

"Don't threaten him," Jared snapped. "I've had enough of you, too. If you want this to turn into a screaming match, we'll arrest the kids right now and have them down at the courthouse for public arraignment in two hours."

"After we've had time to alert the local media, of course," Mel added.

Jared bit his lip to keep from laughing at the murderous look on Tim's face.

"Officers, I don't think that will be necessary," Lexie's attorney said. "I ... can we please have a minute to discuss a few things in private with our clients?"

"Sure," Jared said, shuffling his file back together. "When we come back in this room, though, either they're going to have the answers we want or we're arresting them. Those are their options."

"Give us twenty minutes."

· · ·

HARPER EYED the closed guidance counselor's office door at the high school, frustrated and annoyed that she found herself in the unenviable position of having to go to Jim Stone to ask for a favor.

The idea came to her the previous night in her sleep – where all of her ideas appeared to sprout since she'd started sleeping complete nights pressed against Jared's side – and now that she had gotten it into her head, she saw no other way out of her predicament.

She raised her hand and knocked, meeting Jim's surprised eyes through the glass. He motioned for her to enter, leaning back in his chair as he forced a tight smile.

"You're not going to set me on fire, are you?"

Harper sighed. It was inevitable that they would have to talk about their past before she could make sure that Derek's ghostly future was secure. "Not today."

Harper closed the door behind her and took one of the chairs across from Jim's desk. He seemed nervous, something that thrilled her, but his stance was amiable as he waited for her to begin. When she didn't, he shifted in his chair. "Did you want something specific?"

"Are you sorry for what you did to Zander?" Harper asked, taking herself by surprise when she asked the question. She hadn't been alone with Jim Stone since she kicked him in his special place senior year. He'd tried to approach her several times, but always in a crowd, and now that it was just the two of them she found she needed answers.

"I am very sorry for what I did to Zander," Jim said, sighing heavily. "That's the worst thing I've ever done in my entire life. I've tried to figure out a way to make it up to him ever since, but … I don't know what to do."

"You could tell the truth."

Jim balked. "To who? Zander is an adult. It's too late to get him into gym class."

"You could tell everyone in this town that you lied," Harper suggested. "You could tell them what a snake Dominic was – and I'm sure still is. You could tell them that Zander didn't do any of the things you guys accused him of doing."

"Zander has already won," Jim pointed out. "Everyone in this town loves him. Do you see Dominic? He's gone. No one misses him. Look at me? I'm a guidance counselor, one of the lowest paying jobs in existence. I've spent years trying to make sure what happened to Zander never happens to another student here.

"I'm sorry for what happened," he continued. "I'm ... sorry you were upset. I covered for you. Don't you remember that? You could've been expelled for what you did. I tried to protect you because of Zander."

"I wouldn't have cared about being expelled," Harper said matter-of-factly. "It would've been worth it."

"Zander is lucky to have you."

"I'm lucky to have Zander," Harper countered. "Jared says you're sorry, although when I told him what you did he wasn't keen to sing your merits again. Hating you takes a lot of energy. Zander wants me to let it go because he hates being reminded of it."

"What do you want to do?"

"I don't know," Harper said. "I want to believe that you were a misguided kid who handled everything in the worst possible way and that you truly regret it."

"I do."

"Well, then I guess we should let it go," Harper said.

Jim smiled. "Really? Does that mean you'll go out with me?"

Harper made a face. "Seriously? I can't believe you just asked me that."

"I'm joking with you," Jim said, chuckling. "Too soon?"

This time Harper couldn't help but return his smile. "You might want to move a little slower," she suggested. "I can hold a grudge for a really long time."

"I've noticed," Jim said. "So, other than telling me what a jerk I was in high school, did you have another reason for stopping by today?"

"I do," Harper acknowledged, her blond head bobbing. "I need to ask you a few questions about Derek Thompson."

Jim stilled. "Are you working with the police on his death investigation?"

"We're ... collaborating," Harper hedged. "In fact, Jared and Mel have Brandon, Lexie, Dylan, and David at the police station right now. They're either going to fess up to what really happened that night or be arrested."

"Do you think they were involved?" Jim leaned forward, intrigued. "I have to be honest with you, I've never considered any of those kids dangerous. Lexie has certain narcissistic tendencies, but I'm hoping she'll outgrow them once she gets out of Whisper Cove."

"I don't know if they're really murderers," Harper said, opting for honesty. "I do know that they were up to no good. Derek wasn't a bad kid. He wasn't a good kid, but he wasn't terrible either. I think they all got in over their heads and something terrible happened that none of them were expecting."

"Like what?"

Harper pressed her lips together, briefly worried she was about to take a huge step out on a very shaky limb. Ultimately it didn't matter if Jim thought she was crazy, she realized. Derek's soul was more important.

"I think they might've gotten involved with the wrong person," Harper said, choosing her words carefully. "I think they were selling drugs."

Jim's mouth dropped open. "I ... where did you get that idea?"

"It's just something I've been going over in my head," Harper lied. She didn't want to admit what tipped her over to what she believed to be the truth ... not yet, at least. "Can you check and see how many of them were drug tested and what company did the testing?"

"I guess," Jim said. "That's a weird request, though."

"It would go a long way in making me feel better about you," Harper said, guileless. She wasn't above using Jim's guilt to her own advantage. "I have a hunch."

"Well, I guess I owe you," Jim said. "Sit still. I'll pull everyone's files."

TWENTY-TWO

"I'm going to be late tonight," Jared said, holding his cell phone to his ear as he watched the energetic arguing from outside the conference room. "I think we're finally going to get some answers, but I have no idea how long this is going to take."

"That's okay," Harper said, rummaging through her purse to find her keys next to her car in the school's parking lot. "I may have an idea on that front, too."

"What's your idea?"

"I think they were selling drugs."

Harper's pronouncement took Jared by surprise. "Why do you think that?"

"Well, there's a few things that have cropped up since this all started," Harper said. "First off, Lexie goes on and on about clothes and money ... and you mentioned that Jim said her father greased the wheels for her to get in at Western State even though she didn't have great grades."

"Right."

"Lexie's father is Max Studebaker," Harper explained. "He works in pharmaceutical sales, but they're not rich. They're certainly not rich enough for the sandals Lexie was wearing that day at the school.

Those cost more than seven hundred dollars, and I only know that because Zander was drooling over them in a catalog two weeks ago."

"Seven hundred dollars?" Jared was stunned. "Who would spend that much on shoes?"

"Zander would if he made that much."

Jared chuckled. "Maybe she got them on sale or something," he suggested. "She could've picked them up at a garage sale."

Harper snorted. "You know nothing about shoe sales," she said. "There's no way anyone would let those go at a garage sale. Plus, they're new. They were from this season's collection."

"And you're saying her father couldn't afford to buy her those shoes."

"The Studebakers do okay for Whisper Cove, but they're not rich," Harper said. "I have no idea how Max Studebaker could afford to pay off Western."

"Okay, that's a good tip," Jared said. "I still don't see how that leads to drugs."

"It's not one little thing that led me to this," Harper said. "It's quite a few little things. All of the kids were in summer school together ... except for Derek. That suggests they were all mucking up in school. The Thompsons make a decent living, too, and yet Derek was wearing really expensive Nikes. I don't think his parents bought those for him.

"David wears a really expensive watch that I think costs more than a thousand bucks," she continued. "His father sells real estate in a small community. How do they afford that?"

"Is it all about the expensive items?"

"We know they were hanging around the woods on a regular basis," Harper said. "We know they were causing trouble whenever they could because they were popular and thought they could get away with it. We know Derek was drunk and fighting with the other kids. We also know Derek doesn't want to tell us what he was doing with those kids. I think that's because he doesn't want to sully his own memory."

"I understand what you're saying," Jared said. "I just don't see how you've jumped to this conclusion."

"I can't explain it," Harper admitted. "It's something I ... feel. I'm at the high school right now because I wanted to confirm a hunch. Jim Stone pulled all the drug tests for the kids and they were all done by Max Studebaker."

Jared frowned. "You went to Jim Stone on this before telling me?"

"I didn't want you to laugh at me."

"I would never laugh at you," Jared said. "Not about something like this. Is Jim still alive or did you set him on fire?"

"We had a talk."

"And?"

"And I'm going to try not to hate him so much," Harper said. "I can't guarantee it, but he says he's sorry and would take it back if he could."

"I'm glad, but don't force yourself to do something you're not ready to do," Jared said. "I'm sorry about being late tonight. I'd still like to see you ... even if it means just climbing into bed with you and curling up next to you by the time I get out of here."

"There's a key in a hidden box under the railing on the front porch over by the rocking chairs. Let yourself in. I'll get you a key of your own as soon as I can."

"That's pretty progressive," Jared teased.

"Yeah, well ... I guess that's where we're at," Harper said, smiling at the happy tone of Jared's voice.

"Good," Jared said. "I don't know what to do about this drug theory of yours. The money is a concern and there are some interesting dots being connected. I'm not sure you're right, but I think I've learned that it's unwise to bet against you. I'll keep you informed if we get anything on this."

"Okay," Harper said. "I'll be waiting for you when you climb into my bed."

"I'll be there as soon as I can. You can trust me on that."

Harper disconnected and returned to her key hunt, her grin mischievous as she thought about different ways to surprise Jared when he crawled into bed with her. She grew frustrated when she couldn't find her keys, and when Jim approached from behind she practically jumped out of her skin.

"You scared me!"

"I'm sorry," Jim said, holding up his hands. "Is something wrong?"

"I can't find my keys," Harper said. "I think I dropped them or something."

"Do you want to go back and look in my office? I've locked the school up, but I'll open it back up for you."

"That's okay," Harper said, shaking her head. "I have a spare set at home. I can call Zander to bring them to me."

"I have a better idea," Jim said. "How about you let me give you a ride … and maybe buy you dinner … and then we can talk about everything and really put it in the past. I would like that."

Harper wasn't sure she was up for that. "I don't know."

"They're having a fish fry out at Benny's Pub," Jim offered. "It's close to town and it's very low key. I promise I don't have ulterior motives."

Harper blew out a sigh. "You know what? That sounds great. It will save Zander a trip and if I'm really going to forgive you, I guess I should hear what you've been up to for the past ten years."

"Great," Jim said. "It's a date."

"WHERE ARE WE AT?" Mel asked, opening the door to the conference room and fixing the inhabitants with an expectant look.

"We want to talk deals," Tim said, his shoulders slouched.

Mel ran his tongue over his teeth and exchanged a look with Jared. "No deals."

"But …."

Jared held up his hand to quiet the room. "It's time you people took responsibility for your actions," he said. "That means everyone. If you cooperate, we'll put a good word in for you with the judge. If not … you're on your own."

"This is all Derek's fault," Lexie hissed.

"Shut up, Lexie," David snapped.

"You shut up!"

"Both of you shut up unless you're going to provide us with answers," Jared instructed, returning to his seat. "Before we do that, though, I want to ask about the drugs you've been selling." He was playing a Harper's hunch, and although he hadn't gotten a chance to mention it to Mel, the older police officer kept his face blank instead of showing shock.

"How did you know about that?" Brandon asked, dumbfounded.

"I don't think the fact that David is wearing a watch he couldn't possibly afford otherwise, and Lexie walks around in expensive shoes her parents can't afford while not holding down a job was a smart move on your part," Jared replied, internally reminding himself to reward Harper with something special when he finally got a chance to reunite with her. "Talk."

"This wasn't our idea," Dylan volunteered. "Derek was the one who started it and he brought us in after the fact."

"I'm assuming you've been getting some of your product from Lexie's father," Jared said, acting as if he'd been sitting on the information instead of recently gleaning it from his girlfriend. "We know that Max Studebaker fudged all of your drug tests. I'm guessing Derek wanted to date Lexie to get access to her father's stash, because he certainly didn't seem to like her."

"No one likes her," Brandon said. "We didn't have a choice, though."

"How long has this been going on?" Mel asked.

"We started last summer," David supplied, earning a murderous look from his father. Jared guessed Tim wasn't aware of all of his son's shenanigans. "Derek approached us when we were partying by the river and told us he found a great way to make extra money."

"It was just pot at first," Dylan said. "None of us were keen on doing it, but Derek was flashing huge wads of cash and … well … we wanted in."

"This town sucks," Lexie added. "We needed the money so we could get out of here. You really can't blame us."

"Yes, that's exactly what I was thinking," Jared said dryly. "Where was Derek getting his product?"

"We didn't know at first," Brandon replied. "He wouldn't tell us. He was all 'it's a secret and you guys haven't earned the secret yet' about it. He was so annoying."

"You found out eventually, though," Jared said. "Who was it?"

Brandon and Dylan exchanged one last look and then gave in, resigned to their fate.

"Mr. Stone."

Jared froze, his stomach churning as he exchanged a look with Mel. "Jim Stone?"

Brandon nodded. "Derek told us that Mr. Stone blackmailed him to start moving product through the school after he caught him ... um ...."

"What?" Mel prodded.

"Derek was gay," Lexie interjected, rolling her eyes. "No one was supposed to know. He hid it well. He boasted all the time about nailing chicks – and he did sometimes because he didn't want to be gay and he thought that would turn things around for him – but he was really into dudes."

Jared's heart sank. "Jim Stone found out Derek was gay and black-mailed him into selling dope?"

Lexie nodded. "I had to pretend to be in love with Derek to cover for him," she said. "It worked well for me because Derek was so popular and he didn't expect sex from me. Mr. Stone approached me to help because my father was always bringing samples home and he never kept track of them like he was supposed to. I had to steal samples and give them to Mr. Stone so he could cut them into stuff we could sell to the kids."

"What kind of stuff?"

"Mostly uppers," Brandon answered. "No one wants a downer other than pot."

"What did you do in the woods?" Mel asked.

"That's where we usually partied and made arrangements to trade off with other kids," Dylan said. "We got to keep fifty percent of the profit and we turned the other fifty percent over to Mr. Stone."

"What happened with Derek? Why did you kill him?"

"We didn't kill him," David balked. "Mr. Stone wanted a meeting with Derek because he was making noise about wanting to quit and enjoy the summer before going to college. Mr. Stone didn't like that. He told me to call him and get him out to our regular party spot."

"We thought he just wanted to talk to him," Brandon said.

"We all went out there and had a few drinks … and we were having a good time … and then Lexie opened her big mouth," Dylan said. "She told Derek that Mr. Stone was coming and he got scared. It started this big fight with everyone and she threatened to out him if he didn't tow the line for the rest of the summer."

"Derek told her to shut up and he was getting ready to leave when Mr. Stone showed up," Brandon explained. "We'd been fighting for a few minutes and lost track of time … mostly because we were all pretty drunk."

"What did Stone do?" Jared asked, already knowing the answer.

"He started berating Derek and calling him names," David replied. "He called him a faggot and some other stuff and told him he was an abomination against nature. Derek tried to push him to get away … he was crying … and that's when Mr. Stone just lost it."

"He grabbed one of our beer bottles and slammed it into Derek's head," Lexie volunteered. "Derek just stood there for a moment … kind of like he was dazed … and then he fell over."

"We all thought he was just knocked out," David supplied. "Mr. Stone was ranting and raving and kicking beer bottles around. He kept going on and on about how Derek was going to ruin everything for him."

"When did you realize Derek was dead?"

"It was late," Brandon answered. "We were getting ready to leave and he still hadn't woken up. Mr. Stone left us to take care of him. He told us to make sure Derek realized that leaving wasn't an option when he woke up. The problem is … Derek never woke up."

"When we realized he was dead we kind of panicked," Dylan

admitted. "We were going to leave him in the woods and run, but we knew other kids in the area knew where we partied and that would be traced back to us."

"We carried him to the park and put him close to the merry-go-round," David said. "We thought people would think he was drunk and fell into it and accidentally died. We didn't think anyone would realize he was … ."

"Murdered?" Jared asked, cocking an eyebrow.

"Pretty much," David said. "We never meant for any of this to happen. You have to believe us."

"I'm a good girl," Lexie said, crossing her arms over her chest.

Jared pushed himself to his feet and glanced at Mel. "Let's talk outside." He fixed the teenagers with a dark look before walking out of the room. "I'd get comfortable if I were you. We're going through all of this again when we get back."

"What's going to happen to us?" Brandon asked.

"I honestly have no idea."

TWENTY-THREE

"So, tell me about yourself," Jim said, leaning back in his chair and wiping his hands on his napkin.

"You know me," Harper said, dipping a French fry in ketchup. "We live in a town the size of a postage stamp. There's not much to tell."

"Oh, I don't believe that," Jim said, smiling as he watched her. For some reason, he reminded Harper of the shark from *Jaws* for a moment. She tried to shake the worry niggling the back of her brain, but it refused to go away. "People talk about you all the time."

"I'm sure they do," Harper said. "I'm kind of ... over it."

"Over it?"

"That's what I said," Harper replied, her hackles rising. "I used to care what people thought about me and now I just ... don't."

"Oh, now, let's not start a new fight," Jim suggested. "I'm just trying to get a feel for how your life is. You were always kind of a loner in high school."

"I wasn't a loner," Harper corrected. "I had Zander."

"Yes, you two were joined at the hip," Jim said. "Are you still tight? I mean, I know you are. I hear you two even live together. Is he still the love of your life, or has the cop taken his place?"

"He's my best friend and he always will be," Harper said, narrowing her eyes.

"Does that mean you'll always live together?"

"No."

"Are you going to move in with the cop ... what's his name again?" Jim asked.

Harper was uncomfortable with his keen interest. "Jared," she supplied. "We haven't been dating long enough to move in together. If it becomes an issue down the line we'll deal with it then."

"And he doesn't mind sharing you with Zander?"

"I think Zander is the one sharing me with him," Harper clarified. "Jared and Zander get along. They like each other. I'm not worried about them having a fight over me. It's kind of a ludicrous thought."

"But Zander has never wanted to share you with anyone," Jim pressed. "I know when I asked you out way back when that he had a fit."

"He did not."

"Of course he did," Jim argued. "That's why you wouldn't go out with me. Are you going to deny it?"

Harper was starting to tire of Jim's attitude. "I didn't go out with you because of what you did to Zander," she said. "He never told me not to go out with you. He wouldn't do that. I didn't want to go out with you because I was pretty sure you were a skeezy jackass. I'm starting to think that again."

"You're so testy," Jim teased, making a face. "I'm merely asking questions in an attempt to get caught up on your life. I didn't realize that was against the law."

"No, you're suggesting that Zander somehow has control over me," Harper countered. "He doesn't have control over me. We're friends."

"Okay," Jim said, holding his hands up in a placating manner. "I'm sorry I upset you. Trust me. That's the last thing I want to do."

Harper wasn't so sure. Jim's demeanor was ... sketchy. That's the only word she could come up with to describe it. "Well, thank you for dinner and the catch-up session," she said. "We should really be going.

Zander will be waiting for me at home and I'm supposed to spend the night with Jared. I would hate for him to start looking for me."

"You really like him, huh?"

"I really do."

"Okay," Jim said, a pleasant mask moving over his face. "Just let me pay and we'll get out of here."

"Thanks."

"**WE** NEED to let the prosecutor sort out these charges," Jared said, going over the signed confessions in his hand as Mel poured a mug of coffee. "I don't even know what to think about all of this."

"We also need to process all of the kids and put them in holding cells for the night," Mel said. "They can't be arraigned until tomorrow morning now, and I'm not risking letting any of them out of here in case they bolt."

"I agree," Jared said. "Do you want to be the one to tell them, or should I?"

"Oh, please let me do it," Mel said. "I want to see Tim's face when I slap the cuffs on David."

"I know you don't like him – and I really don't blame you – but I don't think he knew about the drugs," Jared offered. "I think he suspected his son covered up Derek's death. I think he thought one of the other kids did it and David accidentally found himself in a bad situation."

"I think he's a jerk," Mel said.

"He's definitely a jerk," Jared agreed. "I ... ." He didn't get a chance to finish his statement because the sound of the bell over the outside door caught his attention. When he shifted in that direction, he found Zander striding toward him. "What's up?"

"What's up with you?"

"Um ... we're in the middle of a murder investigation," Jared replied, nonplussed. "Why are you here? I thought you would be home with Harper."

Zander made a face. "I thought she was here with you," he said. "I went looking for her when she didn't come home. I figured she was at your place. Jeff is settled in nicely above the garage, by the way. I took him burgers."

"That was nice of you," Jared said. "Why would Harper be with me? I told her I was working late."

"When?"

"I called her about three hours ago," Jared replied. "I knew this was going to run late and I didn't want her waiting up for me. She told me where your extra key was so I could let myself in later."

"Oh, you guys are so cute you can't even be away from each other for one night," Zander said, rolling his eyes. "If she's not with you, where is she?"

"I don't know," Jared answered, racking his brain. "She was at the high school when I called her, but she was leaving."

"Why was she at the high school?"

"She's the one who came up with the drug theory, isn't she?" Mel asked. "I thought it was weird you came up with that out of nowhere and nailed those kids with it. It appears you're not the genius I thought you were. Harper is."

Jared's smile was sheepish. "She did float a theory by me."

"That's great," Zander snapped. "Why did she go to the high school?"

"I'm not exactly sure," Jared replied, his stomach twisting as realization set in. "She said she wanted to talk to Jim Stone and check on the drug tests administered to the kids. Holy crap."

Mel and Jared exchanged a worried look.

"What's wrong?" Zander asked.

"I didn't even think about it because she said she was leaving the school when I called," Jared said. "I ... we have to find her right now." He started moving toward the front door.

"What is going on?" Zander asked, frustrated. "Where is my Harp?"

"Jim Stone has been using the kids at the high school to sell drugs," Mel explained. "We just got their confessions and they all fingered him."

"He's also the one who killed Derek Thompson," Jared said, throwing open the door but not walking through it. "He has Harper."

"You don't know that," Mel said. "You said yourself she was leaving."

"To go home," Jared exploded. "I thought she was safe at home with Zander all this time. I ... where would he take her?"

"Maybe the kids know," Mel suggested.

Jared stormed back through the building. "If he hurts her, I will hunt him down and kill him with my bare hands."

"I THINK you're going the wrong way," Harper said, keeping her voice even as she stared out of the window of Jim's car. They were supposed to be heading back toward Whisper Cove. Instead, Jim blew right past the road that led to the downtown area and kept going farther out. They were on the far side of town, and Jim was speeding like a maniac.

"I know where I'm going," Jim replied, his eyes focused on the road. He gave all appearances of being relaxed, but Harper's inner danger alert pinged to tell her she was in real trouble.

"My house is back the other way," Harper said, hoping she didn't sound shrill. "I'm really tired and I need to get home. Jared will be looking for me."

"God, is that all you talk about?" Jim asked. "Jared this and Jared that. When it's not Jared it's that fruit Zander monopolizing the conversation."

Harper scowled. "You haven't changed a bit."

"I never said I did," Jim said.

"You said you regretted what you did to Zander," Harper charged. "You don't regret it. You're a bigot ... and an asshole, for that matter. Turn around and take me home."

"I did regret what I did to Zander," Jim countered. "It kept me from you, so of course I regretted it."

"Take me home!"

"Shut your mouth," Jim snapped. "There's no reason to scream."

Harper wasn't so sure. She glanced over her shoulder, the darkness swallowing the road and leaving everything blank. There wasn't even another car in the general vicinity. She inadvertently jumped when Derek popped into view in the back seat. She opened her mouth to say something and then snapped it shut. Now was not the time to tip Jim off about Derek's ghost.

"You need to get out of here," Derek said, his voice raspy. "I remembered what happened to me."

Harper pressed her eyes shut briefly before turning to Jim. "You killed Derek Thompson, didn't you?"

Jim was taken aback. "Why would you ask me that question?"

"Because you did it," Harper said. "Why?"

"I think you're confused," Jim said, turning his eyes back toward the road. "You should probably just sit there and be quiet. I think we both would prefer that."

"I was running drugs for him," Derek explained. "He blackmailed me into doing it for him because he found out I was gay. It seemed like the worst thing in the world when he threatened to out me. I guess that's not true, is it?"

Harper felt sick to her stomach. "You blackmailed Derek into selling drugs for you," she spat. "He was gay and instead of helping him you threatened to out him."

"Who told you that?" Jim hissed.

"I figured it out on my own."

"That's a lie," Jim said. "If you knew that you wouldn't have gotten in a car with me. If you knew that you wouldn't have come to the school today. Someone told you. Who?"

Harper opted to go with the truth. "Derek told me."

"Derek is dead," Jim shot back. "He didn't tell anyone outside of his little circle because he was terrified of being judged. He was a faggot and he didn't want anyone to know it. I don't blame him."

"You're just … horrible," Harper said, her eyes glued on the murky scenery as it flew by the car window. They were moving too fast for her to attempt a jump. "You're the one who spearheaded the movement against Zander in high school, aren't you? You only used

Dominic as a scapegoat, and he was too dumb to see what you were doing."

"Yeah, Dominic was an idiot," Jim agreed, chuckling. "I thought if we made things rough enough for Zander he would switch schools. That would've left you all alone and in need of consoling. It didn't really work out that way, did it?"

"I hope you die."

"Don't push me, Harper," Jim warned. "I don't want to hurt you, but you're not leaving me many options here."

"Where are you taking me?"

"To a safe place," Jim replied, the corners of his mouth tipping up. "You're going to like it there."

"He has a cabin out in the middle of nowhere," Derek said. "If he gets you out there you'll never leave. You have to try and escape now."

Harper had already figured that out on her own. She narrowed her eyes at the approaching intersection, hope flaring. She knew where they were ... and she knew exactly how to escape if he would slow the car.

She carefully undid her seatbelt, keeping her eyes fixed forward. She was thankful Jim was driving fast enough that the rough road absorbed the sound of her undoing the seat belt. She held it in place to give the illusion it was still fastened ... and then waited. They were almost at the intersection and it was a four-way stop. Jim was going to have to slow down at the very least.

"You're never going to get away with this," Harper said. "Jared knows I was at the school with you today."

"I don't believe you. You're making that up."

"I was on the phone with him right before you showed up by my car," Harper said. "I ... you stole my keys, didn't you?"

"Guilty," Jim said, grinning. "I took them when you were in the bathroom. I wanted to have some time alone with you."

"Well, that worked out well for you," Harper said. "Now I hate you more than I ever did and Jared knows what you've done."

"Jared doesn't know anything," Jim said.

"All those kids were in the precinct today. They either had to confess or go to jail."

"On what evidence?" Jim asked. "The cops in this town couldn't find their own asses with both hands. They've got nothing on any of us."

"They've got more than you realize," Harper countered. "I wasn't lying before either. Jared knew I was at the school with you. He'll come after you ... and he'll kill you."

"I think you're overestimating your worth," Jim said. "Jared has known you for a month. I've known you for most of my life. Who do you think wants you more?"

Jim lifted his foot from the accelerator and the car started to slow.

"I think Jared wants me more," Harper replied, readying herself. "I also think he's definitely going to kill you." She didn't give thought to what she was about to do, instead throwing the door open and flinging the seat belt off as she rolled to the side and out the door.

Jim realized what she was attempting at the last moment and tried to speed up, but it was already too late.

Harper hit the ground hard, the force of the collision knocking the breath out of her. She pushed herself to her feet, her hip screaming in protest. Derek appeared on the street next to her and together they watched Jim slam on the brakes.

"He'll come back for you," Derek warned. "He'll kill you now, just like he killed me."

"He'll have to catch me first," Harper said, turning toward the woods and forcing herself to break into a run despite the pain. "I have the upper hand out here. I know exactly where I'm going. Come on!"

TWENTY-FOUR

"This isn't good," Jared said, his heart hammering as he looked over Harper's abandoned car. "She wouldn't just leave her car here for no good reason. Stone has to have taken her."

Zander's face was grim. "I'll kill him if he touches her."

"You're going to have to get in line," Jared said, shifting to look over his shoulder at the spot Mel paced while talking on his cell phone. "Who is he talking to?"

"My mother."

"Why?" Jared was beyond frustrated.

"Because if anyone in this town has seen Harper in the past few hours, my mother will find out," Zander replied. "I . . . ."

Jared's phone dinged with an incoming call, and when he glanced at the screen he was almost overwhelmed with relief. He pressed it to his ear. "Harper? Where are you?"

Zander moved closer, excited. "Tell her I'm going to kill her for scaring me like this."

Jared held up his finger to quiet Zander as he listened. Zander was horrified when he saw Jared's relief turn to anger . . . and then outright fear. "Where are you now?" He listened. "Keep going toward my house. We're on our way. I have Mel and Zander with me. Whatever you do ... keep your head down. If you have to hide in the woods and can't make it to the house, I'll come find you. I ... wait!"

Jared was anguished when he pulled the phone away. "She jumped out of Jim's car and is in the woods behind my rental. She's still at least a mile away, but she wanted me to know that if something happens to her, Jim is the one who did it."

"Come on," Zander said, striding in the direction of Jared's car. "Don't get morose. Harper is tough and strong. She bested Jim once before. I hope she kicks him in the balls again."

Jared continued to stare at his phone a moment, hoping it would ring and Harper would tell him she was okay. "I can't lose her."

"You're not going to lose her," Zander snapped. "Suck it up. She needs us."

Jared snapped out of his reverie and jogged toward his cruiser. "I'm seriously going to snap that guy's neck."

"Now you're going to have to wait in line," Zander said.

HARPER'S CHEST heaved as she bent over to catch her breath, leaning her head against a tree and listening to the sounds of the forest around her in case Jim made his presence known. He was behind her, Harper managing to put a good amount of distance between them before he hopped out of his car and followed her into the trees. She had no idea where he was now.

"How close are we to your boyfriend's house?" Derek asked, glancing around. He whispered even though Jim couldn't hear him.

"I don't know for sure," Harper admitted, her voice low. "I have a general idea where we are, but I think we meandered around a little bit. I might be turned around."

"That's not the best way to stay alive."

"I'm sorry my terror and panic have been inconvenient for you," Harper muttered.

"You shouldn't have stopped to call your boyfriend," Derek chided. "We lost time."

"I had to make sure he knew what was going on in case ... ." Harper didn't finish the sentence. She didn't have to. If anyone knew what worried her, it was Derek. "Do you remember how he killed you?"

"He hit me in the head with a beer bottle," Derek replied. "I don't remember anything after that. I'm not sure if I died right away or hung on a little bit. I guess it doesn't matter now."

"You've got a hard head," Harper said, straightening and staring out into the darkness. "I'm surprised that killed you." She was going for levity, but it sounded lame. Any head injury could kill someone. "I shouldn't have said that. I'm sorry."

"It's fine," Derek said. "I did have a hard head. You still have your hard head in place. We need to keep it that way."

"Why are you trying to help me?"

"Because you tried to help me even though I wasn't ready to listen," Derek answered. "You're a good person and you don't deserve to die. I was a bad person."

"You didn't deserve to die," Harper countered. "What happened to you was … a tragedy. Jim took advantage of your fear and confusion and used you as a weapon. No one blames you."

"I blame me," Derek said. "If I had been strong enough to tell my parents what was going on … ."

"Why didn't you?"

"Because my father looked at me as an athlete and … man," Derek explained. "I didn't want him to stop looking at me that way when he found out I … was different."

Harper's heart went out to him. "He wouldn't have stopped loving you," she said. "He was your father. He might have been surprised at first, but something tells me he would've understood and loved you no matter what. That's what a good father does … and you would only seek out the respect of a good man."

"I'm going to miss him," Derek said.

"You're going to go to a better place," Harper said. "I promise I'm going to help you do it … just as soon as we get out of here and make sure Jim is behind bars. Come on. Jim is out there somewhere and we can't afford to wait here and let him find us."

"Maybe we *should* wait here," Derek suggested. "He's trying to get ahead of us. What if we wait and then turn around and go back to the road? He wouldn't expect that. You might be able to steal his car ... or at least hide close to the road until your boyfriend shows up."

It was an interesting thought, and yet Harper almost immediately discarded it. "What happens if he's waiting for us to do that? I told Jared we were heading toward his place. That's where he'll be."

"What do you think he'll do when he catches Jim?"

"Kill him."

Harper started walking again, trying to keep her feet light as she listened. Derek watched her back as she moved forward, and even though he couldn't do anything to stop Jim, she was thankful for his company.

Moving through the trees when she could barely see a thing – her only landmark being the moon as it periodically peeked through the treetops – was disconcerting. With every step Harper convinced herself she was giving away her position. Every sound caused her heart to jump. Every furtive shadow made her dig her fingernails into her palms and ready herself for an attack. After what felt like forever – she couldn't keep track of real time passing because her mind was a mess – she caught a glimpse of something through the murkiness and pulled up short.

"What do you see?" Derek asked.

Harper almost wept with relief when she realized what she was looking at. She'd taken a more roundabout path than she realized, and instead of coming up to Jared's house at the side like she initially envisioned, she'd almost gone too far. She was looking at the light above his garage. "Jeff."

"Who is Jeff?"

Harper ignored the question and picked up her pace, moving toward the garage with relief. "We're there. We're almost safe."

"Almost," Jim said, moving out from behind a tree close to the garage and cutting Harper off from safety.

"Holy crap," Derek muttered as Harper took an inadvertent step backward. "How did he get ahead of us? I told you we should've gone back to the road. Now look what you did."

Harper ignored him. "You need to go, Jim," she said, her voice even as she tried to pretend she wasn't terrified. "I called Jared. He knows you took me. He's on his way."

"See, you keep saying things like that, and yet I don't believe you," Jim said. "I think you're making it up so I'll think I'm in trouble and run. What you don't seem to understand is that I've been waiting for you for a really long time. I'm not going anywhere without you."

Harper licked her lips as she glanced around. The area was quiet … too quiet. If Jared was here he would be calling for her. She would see police lights. She would hear … something. It was deathly silent.

"Derek told me a few things while we were walking in the woods," she said, changing tactics. "He told me all about your drug operation. He told me how you recruited him first because he was gay and you wanted to blackmail him. He told me how you encouraged him to go after Lexie because of her father's access to pharmaceuticals. He also told me that it was your idea for him to date Lexie because she made a good cover. You're sick and twisted … even more than I originally thought."

"You talked to Derek when?" Jim asked, glancing around. "Derek is dead."

"That doesn't mean he's still not here."

Jim frowned, knitting his eyebrows together as he considered Harper's statement. "People have been saying you can talk to ghosts for as long as I can remember," he said. "Is that what you're trying to tell me? Did Derek's ghost tell you all of these things?"

"He's standing right next to me."

"Really?" Jim appeared amused. "Tell him I'm not sorry he's dead."

"I think he's already figured that out on his own," Harper said. "You're done here, Jim. You know that, right? There's nothing left for you."

"You're here."

"I won't go with you," Harper said. "I'll die first."

"You don't really have a say in the matter, Harper. I'm stronger than you and there's no way out of this."

"I could run back into the woods."

"I'll catch you," Jim said. "You can't take me by surprise this time. Personally, I can't believe you had the stones to jump out of a moving car. That was a bold move. I didn't see it coming. I knew you would try to escape, but I thought that would happen when I got you out to my cabin. I have to give you credit, though. You've led me on a merry chase.

"Unfortunately for you, I've been watching you for a long time," he continued. "I used to stand outside of your house and watch you and your live-in homo watch television together. It was pretty disgusting the way you were always loyal to him. Don't worry, I'll … beat that out of you."

Harper swallowed hard.

"It took me a second to figure out your plan when you jumped out of my car," Jim said. "Then I remembered where your boyfriend lived. I followed you out here the other night, too. You spent the whole night here with him. I'm starting to think you're a slut."

Harper narrowed her eyes. "You've been following me all this time?"

"Off and on," Jim replied. "I've always had a crush on you. I didn't lie about that. I think you and I are going to be happy together … once you have a chance to get all of this rebellion out of your system, that is."

"I'll never go with you," Harper said. "You'll have to kill me."

"You keep saying that, but I think once we've had a chance to bond you're going to change your tune," Jim countered. "I think that spending so much time with Zander has confused you. You'll start thinking straight when we've spent some time together."

"You're just … sick," Harper spat.

"You'll learn to love me," Jim said, taking a step forward. "Now, if you're done playing your ghost games, I think we should get moving. It's going to be a long night and I want to get you settled in your new home."

"Think again," Jeff said, stepping out from behind the garage and taking Jim by surprise as he swung a shovel toward his face.

Jim saw the blow coming and managed to deflect some of it, but the shovel landed on his shoulder hard, causing him to cry out. Harper took advantage of Jim's confusion and scurried away from him, keeping her eyes on Jeff as she gave Jim a wide berth. When she hit Jared's lawn – which really did need a good mow – Harper turned to Jeff and found him grappling with Jim over the shovel.

"Run," Derek instructed. "You have to get away from him."

"I'm not leaving Jeff," Harper snapped.

"You have to," Derek said. "Jim will kill him and then he'll come for you. This is your last shot to get away."

"Like hell," Harper muttered, her eyes landing on the rake leaning against the back of the garage. "I think I know how to turn things in our favor."

JARED SLAMMED his cruiser into park in his driveway, leaving the lights on and hopping out of the vehicle on a dead run.

"Harper!"

Zander and Mel followed, their keen eyes scanning the yard in search of movement.

"She might not have made it back here," Mel said. "The county boys are searching the highway right now. If they find her ... ."

"She's here," Jared said. "She has to be."

"We'll find her," Mel said. "It's just ... that's a long hike in the woods when you're alone and someone is chasing you. Jim could've gotten her. He could've ... ."

"Don't you dare finish that sentence," Jared hissed. "She's here. I'm going to find her."

"I'm with him," Zander said, moving toward the tree line. "My Harp would never leave me. She loves me too much. She's also fond of Jared. I'm still her favorite, though."

Mel rolled his eyes. "I love Harper, too," he said. "I'm just saying ...
."

The distinct sound of scuffling hit their ears and Jared was already running in that direction before Mel could finish what he was about to say. When the trio rounded the corner of the garage, they pulled up short at the sight in front of them.

Jeff had the handle of a shovel wrapped around Jim's neck, holding him in place, and Harper was practically screeching as she took on the struggling man with a rake.

"You're a sick piece of work," Harper yelled. "I think you're disgusting. I think what you did to Derek was horrible. I think what you did to Zander was horrible. I hope they put you in a cell with a big bubba rapist in prison so you can complain about homosexuals to your heart's content."

Jared's eyes widened as Harper lifted her leg and slammed her foot into Jim's groin, causing him to scream and reach for his most precious possession. He went limp as Jeff struggled to hold him steady. Jeff finally relented and watched him fall to the ground, where Jim proceeded to roll and hold his testicles as Jeff watched him with impassive eyes and the shovel at the ready.

"You're a big ninny," Harper said. "I really hate you. I should've set you on fire when we were in high school. I would've been doing the world a favor." She lifted her leg again and slammed it on top of Jim's hands as he tried to protect himself. The man bellowed, his face contorting in agony. "You're a sick pervert and I think you're an ass, too."

"Harper!"

Harper jumped at Jared's voice, swiveling to find three concerned faces staring at her. "He had it coming," she said, refusing to apologize.

Jared swooped in and grabbed her, pulling her in for a tight hug. "You scared me."

Harper returned the hug, relief at being safe overwhelming her as tears finally threatened. "I'm okay. Jeff saved me."

"Jeff is a hero," Mel said, clapping the worried-looking man on the shoulder and circling Jim with a dark look. "Jim here is a murderer and is going to prison for the rest of his life thanks to Jeff and Harper. How does it feel, boy?"

"I'm going to kill you all," Jim seethed.

"Promises, promises," Mel muttered. "When you're done groping yourself you need to put your hands up so I can cuff you. I'm looking forward to your perp walk downtown. We're going to call all the local newspapers and television stations so they'll be there to see it happen."

"I'm not afraid of you!"

"Then you're dumber than you look," Mel shot back, keeping one eye on Zander as his nephew moved closer to his former tormentor.

"I guess karma finally caught up with you, didn't it?" Zander asked, his face unreadable.

"No one cares what you think, faggot," Jim hissed.

"That did it," Harper said, moving to pull away from Jared. He held her close and refused to let her leave his side. "Someone get me some gasoline."

"I've got this one, Harp," Zander said, grinning. He lifted his own foot and brought it down on Jim's groin, taking everyone by surprise. No one moved to stop him, and when Jim screamed a third time it sounded as if he was a wounded animal caught in a trap.

"Was that really necessary?" Mel asked. "He's been kicked in the nuts so many times I've lost count now."

"Harper got to do it," Zander protested.

"I guess you've earned it," Mel said, giving in. "Don't do it again, though. We don't want one of those things to explode before he gets his day in court."

"Yes, sir," Zander teased, leaving his uncle to deal with Jim and moving toward his best friend. "I'm going to yell at you tomorrow about getting in a car with a murderer."

"He stole my keys," Harper said. "I didn't realize he was a murderer at the time."

"I'm still mad," Zander said, grabbing Harper away from Jared, practically daring him to complain with a dark look. "My Harper."

Jared rolled his eyes, although he couldn't help but smile. "We're going to have to learn to share."

"I guess I can live with that," Zander said, pulling Harper to him and burying his face in her blond hair as he let the tears overtake him. "I need her right now, though."

"Take your time," Jared said, smiling. "I'm going to handle your murderous little friend over there. I'm going to want her back in exactly two hours."

"We'll work out a custody arrangement," Zander murmured as Harper rubbed his back.

"Or we'll just all hang out together," Jared countered. "Everything is going to work out. Don't worry about that."

For the first time that night, no one was worried about anything.

TWENTY-FIVE

J ared dropped the small cooler he was carrying on the ground next to the hammock the next afternoon, grinning as he watched Harper relax with her book. She wasn't wearing a stitch of makeup and she was dressed in simple yoga pants and a tank top, and he still thought she was the prettiest thing he'd ever seen.

"Are you going to stand there watching me all day, or are you going to get in the hammock?" Harper didn't glance up from the book.

"I'm coming," Jared said, moving closer and eyeing the roped swing bed. "How do I get in this?"

Harper finally put the book down and graced him with a smile. "Roll in next to me."

It took a little finagling, but Jared finally managed to climb in next to her, sighing when she situated herself so she could rest her face on his chest.

"I was starting to think you weren't coming," Harper admitted after a moment. "How are things down at the station?"

"Jim has officially been charged with Derek's murder, so many drug counts I can't keep track of them all, and stalking and kidnap-

194

ping you," Jared replied, rubbing soft circles on the back of her neck. "Brandon, Dylan, Lexie, and David are all facing drug charges. It looks like the prosecutor is going to offer them a deal for community service and a clean record if they keep their noses clean for five years."

"Are you okay with that?"

"I don't know," Jared responded honestly. "They knew what they did was wrong and I think they're all pretty horrible. Jim manipulated them, though. I'm not sure they would've done any of those things if he wasn't pulling their puppet strings. The only one in that group who had a legitimate defense was Derek … and he's gone. He is gone, right?"

"I sent him on his way last night while you guys were dealing with Jim," Harper answered. "He wanted to see his parents one more time. Zander and I waited for him outside and then … I helped him cross over."

"That's a good thing, right?"

"It is."

"Then how come you sound so sad?" Jared asked.

"Jim was worse than I thought," Harper explained. "He didn't just do something horrible to Zander when he was a teenager. He terrorized Derek and used how he was born as a weapon against him. He's sick."

"Yeah, well, he admitted what he had in store for you to us at the station – although he's denying he said it now and claims we forced him into a confession by beating him – and it wasn't pretty," Jared said. "You were smart to jump out of his car when you did. How is your hip?"

"You can kiss it and make it better later."

"Gladly," Jared said, tightening his arm around her back. "You know you're going to have to testify in court about what happened, right?"

Harper nodded.

"How are you going to explain the Derek stuff?"

"I'm going to say that I told Jim I was talking to Derek's ghost because I wanted to unnerve him," Harper replied. "That's not techni-cally a lie. I was hoping the knowledge Derek was there would scare him off. If they press me on it ... I don't know what I'm going to do. I'll probably tell the truth."

"I think Jim's lawyer would be stupid to go after you, but I can't say for sure that he won't," Jared said. "I'll be there. I'll be with you."

"Are the kids' deals contingent on them testifying against Jim?"

"Yeah," Jared said. "If we're lucky Jim will try to make a deal of his own and not take this to trial. He'll still do at least twenty years, but he'll have the opportunity for parole at some point."

"That doesn't seem fair."

"I know," Jared conceded. "We can only do what we can do, though. I want you safe more than anything else. We'll know more in a few weeks. Until then, I don't want you to worry about this."

"Do I look worried?"

Jared's expression softened. "You look beautiful." He lowered his mouth and gave her a sweet kiss. "Before we get to really hammocking – wait, is that a word?"

Harper shook her head and smirked.

"I like it as a word," Jared said, unruffled. "Before we get to our official hammocking, I do have a spot of good news for you."

"I love good news."

"It seems that Crimestoppers had a reward for the identification and arrest of Derek's murderer," Jared said. "Since Jeff caught him, he's getting the reward."

Harper perked up. "Really? How much?"

"Ten grand."

"That's wonderful," Harper breathed, rubbing her fingers against Jared's muscled stomach. "Does he know?"

"He does," Jared confirmed. "He wants to get his own place so we could be alone at my place. I talked him out of that."

"Why?"

"Ten grand might seem like a lot to him right now, but it will go quickly," Jared explained. "I talked him into keeping the apartment above the garage in exchange for doing my yard work and repairs. We came up with a plan and I think that he can make a go of a land-scaping and snow removal business here. If he stays at my place until he's on firm financial ground, things should work out for him in six months. He almost cried ... and then he agreed."

"I was so relieved when I saw him," Harper said. "I thought Jim was going to get his hands on me until Jeff showed up. I'm so happy for him."

"Jeff saved you," Jared agreed. "He was only at my house because you saved him, though. He recognizes that. I think he's a little smitten with you."

"That's cute."

"He's going to have to get in line," Jared said. "I was smitten with you first."

"I think your spot is safe," Harper teased.

"It had better be," Jared said, glancing around. "Is it just us? Where is Zander?"

"Well, he was feeling so energetic after last night he decided to go and pick up a date to dump later this evening," Harper replied. "I think we're safe for the next twelve hours."

"Good," Jared said, rolling Harper so she was practically on top of him and kissing her again. "Teach me how to hammock."

"You don't hammock," she said, giggling. "You just lay around in a hammock and enjoy the day."

"That's a good start," Jared said. "Let's enjoy today and not worry about anything else. Then, tomorrow, we'll do it again."

"You don't even know if you're going to like being in the hammock yet," Harper pointed out.

"You're here," Jared said. "I'm pretty sure I'm going to love it."

Harper's cheeks reddened. "So you're saying you want to spend the whole day with me?"

"Just for starters," Jared said. "Our adventure, Heart, is just begin-ning. Relaxing in this hammock sounds like the best start ever, though. Don't you agree?"

Harper couldn't think of anything better. "Are you going to cook for me later, too?"

"I put steaks and fresh vegetables in your refrigerator before coming down."

"I think this is going to be a great day," Harper said, kissing the tip of his nose.

"I think this is going to be a great adventure," Jared clarified, tightening his arms around her waist. "Now, come on. Let's hammock."

Made in the USA
Middletown, DE
19 March 2024

51613707R10120